THE BLAZE OF NOON

The Blaze of Noon

A WESTERN STORY

Tim Champlin

THORNDIKE
CHIVERS

This Large Print edition is published by Thorndike Press, Waterville, Maine, USA and by AudioGO Ltd, Bath, England.
Thorndike Press, a part of Gale, Cengage Learning.

LIBRARY OF CONGRESS CATALOGING-IN-PUBLICATION DATA

Champlin, Tim, 1937–
    The blaze of noon : a western story / by Tim Champlin.
      p. cm. — (Thorndike Press large print western)
    ISBN-13: 978-1-4104-3541-5 (hardcover)
    ISBN-10: 1-4104-3541-5 (hardcover)
    1. Gold mines and mining—Fiction. 2. Large type books. I. Title.
PS3553.H265B57 2011
813'.54—dc22   2010049455

BRITISH LIBRARY CATALOGUING-IN-PUBLICATION DATA AVAILABLE

Published in 2011 in the U.S. by arrangement with Golden West Literary Agency.
Published in 2011 in the U.K. by arrangement with Golden West Literary Agency.

U.K. Hardcover: 978 1 445 83698 0 (Chivers Large Print)
U.K. Softcover: 978 1 445 83699 7 (Camden Large Print)

Printed in the United States of America
1 2 3 4 5 6 7 15 14 13 12 11

For my sister, Shirley, with all my love

"O dark, dark, dark,
amid the blaze of noon. . . ."

John Milton (1608–1674)

PROLOGUE

July 14, 1781
La Purisima Concepción
Colorado Crossing
Northwestern-most mission
  of the Sonora Province

"*Padre* Diaz!"

No reply. *Padre* Mathias Moreno rose from his chair in the sacristy of the crude adobe chapel and looked out the open doorway.

A young Franciscan in a brown robe was tethering a gray burro in the shade of the wall.

"Ah, there you are," *Padre* Moreno said. "All packed?"

"*Padre,* I don't think we should start out across the *Gran Desierto* in such weather," Father Diaz said.

"*Hace mucho calor,*" *Padre* Moreno agreed. "But we can remove our robes and wear cooler cotton. Also, we'll travel at night, and

9

our journey will be pleasant enough."

"Perhaps I should stay," the young priest demurred. "I speak a little of the Quechan language. And they've been showing signs of restlessness. We can't expect to gain their confidence and convert them to the true faith if the priests keep changing, and coming and going all the time. We must be a constant presence, a stable influence."

"It's too dangerous to stay among these people by yourself," *Padre* Moreno explained patiently. "You haven't had much experience in mission work. The Yumas will be civilized in time, just as the Pimas have been. We've baptized a few babies here, and solemnized several marriages. We must now let that take root before we press on for more. We'll go back to Caborca, and return in a few months. They'll be ready to receive us then, and we can make further progress, perhaps even guide them in building a decent church and enlarging and extending some irrigation ditches. Besides, we're leaving seven Spanish families who will be a living example for these poor savages. And twenty-five soldiers from the San Ignacio garrison at Tubac will remain to keep order."

"That's what I'm afraid of. The soldiers are arrogant, and beat these Indians for the slightest offense. They seduce the better-looking Indian women. The soldiers act as if these Yumas are their personal slaves. That is not the way to win converts. And the Indians are becoming very resentful."

"It is regrettable, but an atmosphere of discipline must be maintained," *Padre* Moreno said. "The soldiers provide order and structure and law to give these primitive people the framework of civilization so that Christianity can flower."

"Did Christ or the Apostles beat the people they preached to?" *Padre* Diaz asked pointedly. He turned away with a disgusted look, and began to pull off his brown robe, revealing long, white cotton drawers beneath.

"Leave your robe on until we're out of sight of the Indians," *Padre* Moreno said. "These robes are the visible symbols of our spiritual office."

"Sí." Diaz dropped the hooded robe back into place. "Father, let's rest a few hours and start out this evening. They don't call that long road the *Camino del Muerto,* the Road of Death, for nothing."

"Providence will see us through," Moreno replied with a sigh. It would be a long trip if his young assistant did not settle down. He decided to distract the young priest with a surprise. "Besides, we're not starting out on

11

our journey this minute. You know the missions are in constant need of money. I've noticed that even the poorest of these Indians in their brush and mud huts sometimes display ornaments made of tiny gold nuggets. I've made discreet inquiries as to where the gold might have come from. As you know, neither the Yumas nor the Pimas are like the mighty Aztecs who valued gold highly and possessed much of it. Last week, I finally persuaded the two Indians we've baptized with the Christian names of Diego and Bartholomew to accompany us on the first days of our journey and show us the source of this gold. Apparently it wasn't just picked up from the gravel of the river bottom."

Padre Diaz had stepped inside the sacristy where the thick adobe walls kept the air nearly ten degrees cooler. He pushed up the sleeves of his robe. "Then where did they get it?"

"Somewhere in the Castle Dome Mountains, a few leagues east of here."

"Will they allow us to take some of it?"

"I hope to persuade them," *Padre* Moreno said. "The gold will be used for the good of their people, to help pay for the buildings here, and obtain seedlings for orchards, and furnish them with livestock and clothing.

We must never let them think we're taking any of it for ourselves. We've repeatedly emphasized that we're the poorest brothers of Christ and have taken a vow of personal poverty, as did Saint Francis."

"Those soldiers from Tubac haven't taken any such vow."

Moreno nodded. "That's why we must keep knowledge of this gold a strict secret. If it becomes generally known, there will be trouble. Many treasure seekers will flock to this area, and cause more trouble for the Indians. And the Spanish crown will demand their twenty percent tax as well."

Padre Moreno squatted to roll up his blanket from the straw pallet on the hard-packed earth floor. "I'm ready to go, if you have the rest of our things packed. It would be wise to take two burros and load one of them only with kegs of water," he continued. "Even though it would mean one more animal to water, we can replenish our supply in the Tinajas Altas mountains."

"The High Tanks," *Padre* Diaz repeated. "Is it likely they will be dry this time of year? We'll be gambling our lives that those tanks won't fail us."

Padre Moreno shrugged. "Nothing in life is certain. We'll ration our water until we get there, in case those rock hollows are dry."

A dark face appeared at the doorway. "*Padre* . . . boat is ready."

"Thank you, Diego. As soon as we load another animal with water, we will start." Moreno looked out to see a second Indian, with long black hair, wearing only a loin-cloth and moccasins, striding toward the Colorado River where a log raft was waiting to take them across to the east bank.

Two days later the four men broke camp and started up a narrow cañon into the Castle Dome Mountains jutting up abruptly from the desert floor. They traversed the long slant of a narrow cañon that led to vertically tilted slabs of rock several hundred feet above. The slopes were speckled with various species of cacti, and forty yards to one side were thick, cracked layers of black lava where some ancient volcano had spewed forth. *Padre* Moreno wished he had a better knowledge of geology. Scientists were studying the formation and re-formation of the earth's crust, but there was still much to be learned.

The two priests wore straw hats as protection from the sun, and sandals spared their feet from the sharp rocks and heated ground. As *Padre* Moreno watched the brown backs moving up the cañon ahead of him, he wondered again how these Indians were able to withstand the blazing sun on their bare skin without severe burns. Maybe layers of dirt and dust intervened. Or, more likely, many generations of living in this climate had inured their race against the ravages of solar rays. Unsuccessful efforts had been made to introduce clothing to them. At least white shirts to the men. The women seemed already to cover themselves with a degree of modesty.

The night before, around the campfire, with the younger priest translating as best he could, *Padre* Moreno had told Diego that any gold they acquired would be used for the benefit of the tribe. He wasn't sure to what degree these two Yumas grasped the concept of money and the economy of buying and selling, but he knew they did use some system of barter. And they must know that gold was valuable, or they wouldn't keep its location secret. It was shiny, it was malleable, it was durable, and, from what they knew, it was in limited supply — the perfect material for making jewelry.

Padre Moreno felt rested and confident. The two Yumas apparently were making no attempt to disguise their route, or otherwise

15

confuse the Franciscans about the location of the gold — a tribute to the Indians' trust of the priests.

They hiked another mile, each priest leading one of the loaded burros. Finally Diego stopped and indicated they were to leave the animals in the shade of some boulders, and the men would go on. The Indian led the way, climbing what he perceived as a steep trail, but one that *Padre* Moreno could not have picked out. He watched where the Indian put his feet and followed his steps. His breath came in labored gasps, and he was on the point of requesting a rest stop, when the two Indians paused on a narrow ledge.

"This way," Diego said, pointing at a vertical, dun-colored wall. He ducked low and crawled into an opening between two V-shaped slabs of rock. The other three followed. Ten feet in, the opening widened so the men could stand. The blazing sun was only a twilight filtering through some overhead fissures. They paused to let their eyes adjust to the dimness. Moreno breathed deeply of the cooler air.

Then the Indians led the way to the back of the twenty-foot chamber. Diego moved to one side and pointed. A tiny shaft of sunlight slanted down through the gaps in the tilted rock slabs. The light reflected dully off a vein of rotten white quartz. Imbedded in this quartz, like lacy filigree, were webs and strands of pure gold.

Padre Moreno tried not to show his surprise, or to act as if he were venerating this yellow metal as he carefully touched it with his fingertips. It was no illusion.

Diego grunted and stepped forward to chop off a fist-size chunk of the gold-laden quartz with his stone axe. He handed the ore to Moreno for closer examination.

"This rock was molten at one time," *Padre* Diaz said, crouching by the vein. "Forced up from deep in the earth by hot gases. See how it appears to have had bubbles in it?"

Padre Moreno was surprised. What were they teaching besides theology in the seminaries of Spain these days?

The vein of quartz was at least two feet wide and of unknown depth. The floor was littered with chips of rock where someone had been hacking at the vein and the rock around it. The Yumas had probably been mining this in small amounts for years.

Padre Moreno was trying to form a request to take some of the gold with them when he heard a scuffling noise behind him and *Padre* Diaz yelled. Moreno started to turn when something struck his temple and

17

he knew no more.

Twenty minutes later Diego and Bartholomew were leading the two burros down the
cañon toward the lower desert. The
Quechans, as they called themselves, carried bloodied stone axes in their belts.

Before they reached their village on the
west side of the Colorado River next day,
their tribesmen had killed fifty whites, plus
two more priests farther upriver at the new
San Pedro y San Pablo de Bicuner mission,
and captured all of the Spanish women and
children. The event came to be known in
history as the Yuma massacre.

CHAPTER ONE

July 6, 1878
Tumacacori Mission Ruins
Arizona Territory

Daniel Mora sensed he was being stalked by the deadliest predator in North America — the Apache warrior.

He shifted the Marlin carbine to his left hand and cat-footed from the cover of a *palo verde* tree across a bright patch of moonlight into the inky shadow of an adobe wall that surrounded the church graveyard. Holding his breath, he listened intently for sounds of pursuit. Nothing — only the thumping of his own heart in his ears. Not even the rustling of mesquite bushes. A westerly breeze had died at dusk, leaving a sluggish blanket of heat smothering the valley. He'd paused at the Santa Cruz River, several hundred yards away, to fill his canteen, then crept in a circuitous route to the protection of the mission wall, moving silently, pausing often, staying in the deep shadows of the desert shrubbery.

Even though he'd parceled out his stamina, he was nearly spent. Two hours before sunset, he'd crossed the unseen border from Sonora, pacing himself with a steady, ground-eating lope that ate up the miles. High desert moccasins, folded down and tied just below the knee, protected his legs and feet from catclaw, prickly pear, and *cholla*. Carbine in hand, a single bandoleer of ammunition across his chest, and a half-full canteen bouncing from a shoulder strap were his only possessions as he'd jogged and walked the last fifteen miles, arriving at the Santa Cruz River just at moonrise.

Over the final dozen miles his feet had been driven by fear. Just at sundown he could've sworn he caught a glimpse of a brown shoulder disappearing behind a sandy hillock fifty yards to his right. But he couldn't be sure. And it was that doubt, growing with the lengthening shadows, that had spurred him on. Adrenaline pumping, lungs heaving, he'd half expected to be downed by a bullet or an arrow at every step.

He knew the Apaches, when stalking prey, could blend into the dun-colored desert landscape like a rattler or a lizard. If they wanted to remain invisible, no white man would ever catch sight of them. That's why Mora began to doubt his eyes. If that flicker of a naked body he thought he'd seen was really a stalking Apache, the appearance had to be deliberate.

Maybe a couple of warriors had bolted the reservation, gotten liquored up on *tiswin,* and decided to ambush a lone white man for sport or vengeance. Sinewy, bandy-legged, and tireless, an adult Apache male in top condition could run all day without tiring. Only the legendary Tarahumaras of Mexico were better distance runners. They called themselves the Raramuris, but, by any name, they were not as war-like as the Apaches, and Mora had nothing to fear from them. In fact, a friendly Tarahumara Indian had recently nursed him back to health from a near-fatal rattlesnake bite. The man knew only a few words of English. While a grateful Mora was preparing to leave the Tarahumara's camp in the Sierra Madre Mountains, his benefactor had uttered only two words, but those words were clear as a silver bell, dire as a crack of thunder. The lean Indian had pointed north toward the border and said: "Apache!" Then he'd swept his arms in an all-encompassing circle and said: *"¡Bandidos!"* The Apache devils were somewhere near the border, and the roving bands of Mexican outlaws could be expected anywhere.

Mora's stomach growled with the sound of a night-prowling cat, and he pressed a hand to his flat belly to stifle the noise that seemed loud in his own ears. A handful of mesquite beans he'd eaten ten hours earlier could not sustain his strength much longer.

"Getting too old for this," he muttered. He was not deluding himself. At fifty-eight, he was well past his prime. But two years alone in the desert had restored his health and vigor and given him the endurance of a man half his age. The sedentary life and strain of civilized living would have killed him by now, he rationalized, as he waited for his breathing and heart rate to slow. Then he crept along the wall until he came to a pile of rocks and adobe bricks that had tumbled down, forming a break in the eight-foot wall. Picking his steps, he climbed noiselessly over the pile and found himself in the abandoned graveyard. He barely glanced at the mounds of rocks and weathered wooden crosses, silvered by the moonlight. The tall, dry grass whispered around his legs as he strode toward the ruins of the mission church bulking up before him. He passed to the side of the unfinished, circular mortuary chapel, then disappeared through the arch of the doorway into the church nave, hoping he wasn't being watched by a pair of hard, obsidian eyes. He was becoming paranoid. But, better paranoid than dead, he reasoned. He paused in the blackness to listen once again, but heard only the sound of his own breathing, and the scuttering of disturbed mice or possibly a kangaroo rat on the stone floor. When his eyes adjusted to the darkness, he saw the shapes of the moonlit windows high in the walls on either side, and a shaft of moonlight lancing through a gap in the roof near the sanctuary. He began to feel safer. If there were any Apaches on his trail, the interior of this church would make a good defensive position. He was still uncertain whether Indians of any tribe fought at night. He fervently hoped it was against Apache belief. But hoping would not keep him alive.

He padded toward the transept and looked left and right. From previous visits, he knew the solid wooden door on his left led to the sacristy, and the gaping arched doorway to the right led out into the moonlight. Since this church was abandoned thirty years before, the wooden pews, doors, altar, pulpit, and choir loft had been appropriated for firewood or building material for other dwellings. Sixty years had passed since

Mexico had won its independence from Spain and secularized the Franciscan missions. The Church had withdrawn the brown-robed priests, and the Mexican government had sold the mission lands into private hands. With the passage of time, the unfinished structure was slowly melting back into the earth from which it was formed. It would take at least another 100 years, he guessed, since only part of the building was made of adobe. The rest, including the foundation, was fashioned of stone, the walls several feet thick. The Franciscans had directed the Tohono O'odham, or Papagos, as the newcomers called them, in building a church that would last. They had brought limestone from quarries thirty miles away, heated it in limekilns, then crushed it into powder to make cement that held these massive walls together.

He turned and made his way to an alcove in the left wall near the front, taking care not to step into any of the holes left by treasure seekers. Did he dare strike a light? It was unlikely a small candle, set deep in a wall niche, could be seen by anyone outside. He placed his carbine on the floor and fumbled in his pants pocket for a block of matches he'd dipped in wax for waterproofing. Since he was afoot, the matches were the only thing, besides his rifle, bandoleer, and canteen, he'd carried away from the Indian's camp. He broke off one of these Lucifers from the block and scratched it against the plaster inside the niche. A sulphurous smell bloomed out with the smoke as it flared up. He touched the flame to a wick in a red glass vigil light in front of a carved, wooden stature of St. Francis of Assisi. In the early 1200s, this man had founded the Order of Friars, the brown-robed Franciscans who, centuries later, succeeded the Society of Jesus — the Jesuits — in Spain's efforts to Christianize the Indians of the New World.

All this went quickly through his mind as he dropped to his knees before the statue. He thrust a hand into his canvas pants and withdrew a small object, placing it at the base of the two-foot statue. The three-inch object was a crude replica of a human forearm. "Carved it out of a root. It was the best I could do with that belt knife," he murmured, as if St. Francis did not understand his silent prayer of thanks. The carving was a *milagro,* literally, a miracle. But the word had taken on the meaning of the object as well. He was not petitioning the saint for strength of arm, but was showing gratitude for the saint's help in curing the snakebite in his left arm, thanking him for bringing the Tarahumara Indian to him just when he might have died from the rattler's venom. As he'd been losing consciousness on the mountain trail, Mora had uttered an urgent prayer to St. Francis. And, when he awoke, he'd found himself under a shady rock overhang and a lean Indian massaging the muscles of the arm down toward the hand. Then his rescuer had made a poultice to draw out the poison from the twin puncture wounds. He recalled the Indian giving him something bitter to drink, but remembered nothing more for many hours.

He pushed back the sleeve of his thin cotton shirt. In the flickering light of the votive candle, the wound and the surrounding tissue appeared swollen and red. But there was no fever in it, and he felt he was out of danger. Whatever the Indian had done had brought him back to health.

Mora said a quiet prayer of thanks to God and St. Francis for bringing him the unknown Indian. They'd done a superb job restoring him; no man in other than perfect health could have covered seventy miles, afoot, in the past three days, living off the desert land.

Was the use of a *milagro* more a superstition than a Catholic sacramental? He'd adopted the custom from his Mexican friends. Surely a carved offering in the form of the affected body part was no different than the use of incense to symbolize the rising of prayers at benediction. He glanced again at the painted wooden figure. Some unknown Spanish artist had sculpted his perception of the saint, giving him very severe features and a pointed black beard. Based on the happy friars he knew, Mora judged the founder of their order had probably been a generous, jovial man in his lifetime.

Focusing his wandering thoughts, he said the Lord's Prayer, then rose from his knees with a groan, staggering slightly. Fatigue was draining strength from him like water pouring out of a canteen. Should he leave the candle burning? No. Tonight, darkness was his friend. Besides, the candle should be saved for the next pilgrim who happened along. He blew it out. Glancing aloft at the unseen beam ceiling, he picked up his carbine and felt his way toward the dark alcove of the baptistery and a good, safe place to sleep. Then he changed his mind. Better to be out in the main church in case he had to make a quick getaway. The moon had moved, and now, through a gap in the roof, was illuminating the concave wall behind the vanished altar. Part of a mural still showed faintly on the wall that was pockmarked with bullet holes. In spite of the damaged interior of the old church, it still gave off a sense of peace and calm.

Mora walked softly to a spot where he would have access to a side door if needed, then lay down on the floor along the base of the wall, his rifle beside him. The worn stones felt cool through his thin shirt. The thick walls and high ceiling kept the interior of the building several degrees cooler than the outside air.

What of the morrow? The first thing was to find food. Then, it was another forty or fifty miles north to the village of Tucson where he'd catch the westbound stage. But how? He had no money — not a penny. And except for his rifle and knife, which he wouldn't part with, he had nothing to trade for stage fare, lodging, or food. His whole outfit had been lost when his loaded burro had shied at the rattler, slipped on loose shale, and tumbled over a sheer 300-foot drop into the cañon. Not even the Tarahumara, who'd saved his life, would attempt a climb into the bottom of that gorge to retrieve the pots and pans and camp gear. The Indian wouldn't risk his life even for the small rawhide poke of dust and pea-size nuggets Mora had laboriously collected the past several weeks while prospecting the Sierra Madre wilderness. He'd indicated by signs and the Spanish word, *"oro"*, that the Indian, whose name he approximated as Quanto, could have anything on the mule. But Mora couldn't tell from Quanto's impassive expression whether or not he understood, or was even interested.

It wasn't his gold and gear that he regretted losing, but rather his burro, Atlas, his closest friend, confidant, and companion for nearly two years. He hoped the fall had killed the burro instantly, so the animal hadn't suffered the agony of broken bones and internal bleeding injuries. Peering from the rocky ledge the next day, he thought the burro, far below, probably hadn't moved after he hit bottom.

Mora had been leading the beast around a bend in the trail when he'd nearly stepped on the thick-bodied diamondback sunning itself. The startled reptile had thrown itself into a coil and struck, hitting Atlas in the foreleg. The burro had squealed and lunged backward, yanking the lead rope from Mora's hand, then plunged over the side. Mora had been thrown flat on his face, and, the next second, the snake struck again, puncturing his forearm. Perhaps Mora was alive now because most of the venom had been injected into the burro.

It all played out in Providence, somehow. He groaned and rolled over, pressing his cheek against the cool floor. He was so tired he could've slept on a bed of nails. Yet, he knew he wouldn't rest well this night. A part of him would stay alert to any danger. It was now that he really missed Atlas. His burro was his guard, his watchman who would bray loudly at any approaching creature, human or animal. With the burro nearby, Mora had always slept soundly. Atlas, his patient, long-eared friend who he'd come to love and value more than any human; Altas, the furry, four-legged creature who could communicate without words; Atlas, who bore a black cross on the gray fur of his back as part of his natural coloring. Mora smiled faintly, recalling a Mexican acquaintance who'd assured him the cross was a reward God had bestowed on the lowly beast because one of Atlas's ancestors had carried Jesus into Jerusalem on the first Palm Sunday.

It was his last thought as he slipped into exhausted oblivion.

Unknown to him, a near naked figure glided noiselessly through the broken archway into the darkness of the church.

30

CHAPTER TWO

Daniel Mora opened his eyes to complete darkness. He had no idea how long he'd been asleep. But apparently the moon had set; no outside light filtered through the gaps in the building.

What had awakened him? Maybe a mouse scampering over his body, he guessed, or some unusual sound. All he knew, as he rolled onto his back, was that he'd been lying on the cool stone floor long enough to stiffen badly. The muscles of his shoulders and legs protested at being asked to shift position. *Body too old . . . trail too long,* he thought, stretching his limbs and staring up into the darkness. *Living* rigor mortis. As a younger man, he'd welcomed the soreness from rough games and exercise. It'd made him feel vibrant, alive. Now it was just pain — an inconvenience that he required longer to recover from. Nature's way of preparing him to crave the long rest of death.

He closed his eyes and was relaxing into a doze when a chirping whistle came from outside. *Some early-rising desert bird, sensing the coming dawn?* He'd never heard that bird call before, and sunup was more than an hour away. He'd sleep a little longer, then be up and moving.

Thump! Clang!

He sprang up at the sound of a scuffle several yards away, snatched his carbine, and jacked a round into the chamber.

"Mora!"

The hoarse whisper sent the hair prickling on the back of his neck. Mora hesitated, heart racing, eyes wide, seeing nothing in the darkness. He crept several feet to his left and flattened his back against the wall, then swept the gun barrel in an arc, contacting nothing.

"Mora!"

He heard shuffling steps and someone breathing.

"Who is it?"

"No shoot!" the voice pleaded.

Mora edged away from the sound until he felt a break in the wall that led to the side door. Then he slipped around the corner and darted toward the faintly visible archway. He would take his chances in the open, and he sprang through the doorway, covering the outside ground quickly, breathlessly. It was deserted. A few faint stars dotted the pre-dawn sky. It was still too dark to see anything but general shapes.

"Show yourself!" He kept his voice low, intense.

"No shoot!" the voice said again from inside. The inflection had a vaguely familiar ring. Then Mora saw a white blob appear in the black doorway. He shivered as if the spirit of St. Francis himself was emerging from the side door of the ruined church. He held the Marlin at hip level, finger tightening on the trigger.

"Mora, no shoot!" the apparition repeated as it came toward him.

Sudden relief flooded over him, and he felt weak. He eased down the hammer and lowered the rifle. It was Quanto, the Tarahumara Indian who'd saved his life. He was wearing a white shirt that was flapping open and had given him the ghost-like appearance. Had he just slipped into the garment in order to be seen and recognized?

"Quanto! By God!" Mora breathed. "You scared hell out of me!"

Dawn was graying objects around them.

The Indian put a finger to his lips for silence. As he drew near, Mora saw a bloody knife in his hand. Quanto pointed toward the church. "Apache!" He spat to one side as if the word had a bad taste. He jerked the edge of his hand across his throat, and Mora understood the sounds of the scuffle. Quanto had descended like a fierce guardian angel to cut down the Apache attacker, saving Mora's life by feet and seconds. That was twice the Tarahumara had averted the hand of death.

After a quick look around, Quanto silently glided away toward the shelter of the mesquite. Mora followed him more than 100 yards into the thick growth before the Indian began to circle back toward the Santa Cruz River. Mora was curious but gave the Indian credit for knowing the situation. From the way Quanto moved, they were not out of danger.

They halted in thick trees at the edge of the stream. Summer monsoons had not yet dumped their floods over the valley to swell the marshy Santa Cruz that was fed by *cienagas* and springs.

"La agua es la sangre de la tierra," he muttered the old saying. "Water is the blood of the land."

Quanto, who apparently understood Spanish, nodded as he gazed around intently.

The saying was certainly true here. Only because of this river had the Jesuits, and later the Franciscans, been able to locate a mission on a former site of a Tohono O'odham village. *Acequias,* small irrigation ditches, had supplied the priests and Indian converts with water to nourish vast orchards and fields that supported the compound. More than 1,000 residents, along with herds of cattle and sheep, were protected by Spanish soldiers located only four miles away at Tubac. Mora wished there were Spanish soldiers nearby now.

A light dawn breeze stirred the leaves of a giant cottonwood. The rustling leaves would mask sounds of anyone approaching. Mora saw and heard nothing unusual, but apparently Quanto's senses were sharper. The Indian crouched and led the way to the marshy edge of the stream. They waded into the water, Mora's moccasins sinking into the soft muck. They pushed their way, waist-deep, into the thick willows; the water was pleasantly cool.

Quanto, leading, let himself sink until only his head was above water. Mora did the same, thinking that he needed a good bath. This would soak the sweat out of his clothing. He was glad his matches were water-proofed with wax, and the cartridges sealed. He knelt on one knee, rifle submerged, his head just out of the water. The reeds were so dense he could barely see Quanto's dark hair and features only three feet away.

They remained motionless for several long minutes as dawn silently filtered through the foliage. Mosquitoes began to whine around their ears. Birds awakened to the new day. He recognized the call of the cactus wren. Through a break in the willows, he saw a killdeer strutting along the riverbank.

He sensed movement and shifted his eyes without turning his head. Two half-naked Apaches, one wearing a red headband, were approaching, pointing toward the ground. The sight of stalking death tensed Mora's stomach. The trackers disappeared behind the thick foliage, but their low, guttural voices were close. They halted where he and Quanto had waded into the marshy stand of willows.

Before Mora could even speculate on their next move, he heard the *clicking* of hammers being drawn to full cock. The serene dawn was shattered by the roar of gunfire. Large-caliber slugs ripped through the reeds near his head. The Apaches were firing blindly into the willows, whooping and laughing as if drunk.

Quanto ducked beneath the surface and Mora saw the surge as the Indian pushed off the bottom toward deeper water. Mora drew a deep breath, submerged, and followed, holding himself under by grabbing the thick reeds at their base and pulling forward, squirming through thick underwater growth, the awkward rifle impeding his progress. He heard the *zip* and *pop* of bullets striking the water all around, their force quickly diminished.

Eyes shut, holding his breath, he kicked and clawed toward the safety of the channel. He knew their bodies were churning up the shallow water, bending the willows and leaving a plain trail for the murderous Apaches to fire at. *Maybe they'll think we're thrashing in our death throes,* he thought. Then he felt the slight tug of a deeper current as the reeds thinned and disappeared.

Heart thumping, he stroked forward, lungs burning for air. How much longer could he hold on before he had to surface and breathe? A kicking foot brushed his face, as Quanto swam ahead of him. Mora slitted his eyelids, but could see only a very faint gray. He stroked ahead with one hand, gripping the cumbersome carbine with the other. But every foot, every yard he made would take him farther out of danger. *Maybe they can see the wake of our swimming bodies in this shallow river,* he thought. He pictured them walking leisurely along the bank, waiting for him to surface so they could blow his head off. The thought made his pulse race, quickening his need for oxygen. Mora decided he'd better be ready to come up shooting. But he'd have to be able to stand on the bottom to brace himself, so he prayed the wet rifle would fire. Remembering there was a shell in the chamber, he thumbed back the hammer underwater.

Quanto's lung capacity was much greater than his own, but Mora forced himself to stay under until he began to see spots before his eyes and his lungs were afire.

Finally he could stand it no longer and let his body's natural buoyancy drift him upward, trying not to splash as his face and head broke the surface. He gasped, filling and emptying his lungs as he quickly scanned the bank. No Apaches in sight. Thick bushes and trees bordered the stream.

He bounced gently along in the chest-deep current for several yards. Then Quanto surfaced ahead of him. The Indian signaled for them to stay in the water and keep going. They waded and drifted in the shallow stream for another quarter mile, scanning both banks, alert to any movement. But they saw no one. Mora began to think the two

Apaches had actually been drunk and had just shot at them for entertainment or sport. But then he thought it odd they'd be drunk at dawn. Maybe they'd been drinking most of the night. The Apache who'd crept into the church was either planning a dawn attack, or rumors of Apaches not fighting at night were false.

Even though the church had been long abandoned and the Blessed Sacrament removed, it seemed almost sacrilegious for a dead body to lie inside while coyotes, wolves, or buzzards came to devour the carcass. Perhaps the two stalking Apaches, believing he and Quanto were dead, had gone back to retrieve the body.

By silent consent they waded ashore at a point where the bank was clear of vegetation. While Quanto's keen eyes scanned the surrounding terrain for any sign of the enemy, Mora shook the water from his rifle as best he could. The desert air would dry it quickly. He made a mental note to clean and oil it when he reached Tucson.

Apparently they were safe for the time. Now Mora took the lead, motioning for Quanto to follow, and started walking north, across the desert, lining up a range of western mountains as a compass reference. Quanto carried a canteen, knife, and nothing else. He was wearing moccasins, tan pants, and a white shirt. A blue headband held his long hair out of his face.

Mora had lost his hat, so ripped a sleeve off his shirt and wrapped it into a makeshift turban around his wet hair as protection from the fierce June sun. He was uneasy in the thick mesquite where he couldn't see far in any direction. Too much danger of ambush. He'd feel much better when they reached open desert, away from the dense chaparral.

They'd traveled a mile when Mora caught sight of the church's unfinished bell tower a half mile to their right as they passed it again. Since their initial flight, they'd nearly circled the compound.

Mora walked swiftly, eyes darting left and right. Suddenly he saw a slight movement and his heart leaped. He swung up the carbine just as an Apache leaped from the cover of an arroyo and fired a revolver. The bullet kicked sand at Quanto's feet, and he dove to one side as Mora's Marlin exploded from hip level. The Apache spun back, dropping his pistol, and staggered out of sight into the wash. Mora dashed to his left, into the mesquite, trying to get down the arroyo farther along to see how many attackers there were. A half minute later he caught sight of two brown bodies disappearing at a stumbling run over a hillock toward the church. One Apache with a red headband was helping the wounded one. Mora recognized the warrior as one of those at the river. Apparently they were the same two assailants.

He looked around. Quanto was crouching beside him, holding the pistol the Apache had dropped. He was blowing sand out of its mechanism. It was an old .36-caliber Colt percussion revolver that had been converted to fire cartridges. Five of the six cylinders were still loaded. By downing the Apache before he could get off a second shot, Mora had saved Quanto's life, partially repaying the debt he owed this Indian.

"Damned good thing most Apaches aren't good shots with handguns," he said, knowing Quanto probably didn't understand him. "Let's go." He jumped up and jogged away, dodging this way and that, finally breaking clear of the dense mesquite to the more open terrain that was dotted with saguaro, Spanish bayonet, and a variety of desert growth.

"I'd bet they won't be after us now," he said over his shoulder.

Quanto was watching their back trail. The Tarahumara likely had more experience with other Indians, but, in brushes with roving Apache bands in the past, Mora had discovered they would not doggedly continue a pursuit or siege if odds didn't favor swift victory. He suspected that, of the three warriors on their trail, one dead and one wounded was enough to discourage pursuit. In the long war of attrition with whites and Mexicans, the various Apache bands were hit-and-run guerilla raiders. Much fewer in number, they couldn't afford to take many losses. He had no idea why these Apaches would be after him; he had nothing to steal except his rifle and ammunition. But that was enough — along with the pleasure of watching another white-eyes die.

He jogged across the relatively flat desert terrain, automatically dodging the thorniest of the desert shrubs, aware that his soaking in the river had softened the hard soles and button toes of the high desert moccasins.

During the next half hour, he felt himself growing less cautious as they put more distance between themselves and the ruined mission with no sign of pursuit.

Suddenly he gasped as a thorn stabbed through the softened rawhide and buried itself in the ball of his right foot. The sharp pain caused him to stumble forward and fall to his hands and knees. He sat up and gingerly pulled off the tall moccasin that was turned down at the top and tied around his calf. A two-inch thorn was extracted with the moccasin, leaving a tiny, purplish hole, throbbing like a toothache.

Quanto was on one knee, hardly winded. Mora reached down and gently squeezed the ball of his foot to force out a few drops of blood. He wiped it off and slid the moccasin back on. The rawhide was drying rapidly. That thorn would probably have penetrated a cavalry boot, he reflected, wondering how much the pain would cause him to favor the foot when they started on.

But for now, they silently consented to take a breather. Quanto stood up and scanned their back trail, then checked the loads in his captured Apache pistol. Since they could barely communicate with words, Mora was left to wonder why this stranger from another culture had taken it upon himself to protect the aging white prospector. The Tarahumaras were a peace loving people he'd been told. But, being forced into the mountains by invading tribes and whites had conditioned them to be tough and resilient. Mora thought Quanto's people would be resentful of any white men who wandered into the rugged Sierra Madre.

As his excitement ebbed, Mora sagged,

completely fatigued. The past three days of traveling afoot in the desert heat, the pre-dawn escape, the near miss in the river, another close call with the stalking Apaches, followed by a half hour of jogging had taken their toll on his middle-aged body. Most of the time he ignored the effects of the creeping years, assuming his mind and iron will could overcome any physical weaknesses. But now he wasn't so sure.

Quanto reached under the flap of his shirt pocket and produced two short sticks of jerky, holding one out. Mora nodded his gratitude to the provident Indian and bit into the river-softened dried meat. Likely goat, but the salty, stringy meat was the most delicious food he'd ever tasted. He tried to eat it slowly and savor it, to fool his stomach into thinking it was full when he finished, since this was all he was likely to have for some time to come.

He sat in the shade of a mesquite, chewing on the jerky and studying the Indian's impassive features. The whiskerless, leathery face might belong to a man of thirty-five — or fifty. Mora wished they could speak to one another. Who was this Indian, anyway? Why had he twice rescued a strange white eyes? Treating him for snakebite was possibly only a humane act one man would do for another. But then to follow him seventy miles as an invisible protector. . . . It made no sense. During more than a half century of living, Mora had never encountered anything like it. He was eager to probe the Indian's motivation. Was it for money? Mora had already made Quanto understand that he could have Mora's outfit and what little gold it contained — provided the Indian could somehow salvage the pack from the dead burro in the bottom of the gorge. Maybe Quanto thought Mora knew the source of much more of the yellow metal, and wanted to find the source. The Tarahumaras were a very poor people. And Quanto had not attempted to retrieve the pack, so he couldn't know what was in it, despite Mora's efforts to tell him.

Mora looked away and chewed the jerky thoughtfully. Maybe the Indian had gone to the trouble of saving Mora from poison, and wanted to protect his investment of time and effort. Perhaps Quanto only wanted a shot at his ancient nemesis, the Apache. To discover the real reason, Mora would have to wait until he could find a Mexican to translate, since Quanto seemed fluent in Spanish, while Mora was not.

They finished their meager snack. Instead of renewing his strength, the jerky had only stimulated Mora's hunger. He was still aching, and extremely tired. He brushed away the small stones and stretched out in the shade.

But Quanto said something and rose to his feet, pointing toward the distant, terraced mountains. Mora reluctantly pushed himself erect and followed as the Indian started off at a brisk walk. Evidently Quanto thought it was too early to rest.

Where was the Indian going? Did he have some destination in mind? Mora was bound for Tucson, more than a day's walk to the north. Currently they were angling slightly to the northwest.

At first, Mora kept an eye out for rabbit or peccary — even a coati mundi — anything he might be able to shoot for food. As the day wore on and he saw nothing, he realized most desert mammals were either nocturnal, or hunted in the late evening and early morning to avoid the heat.

The two men trudged along, mile after mile. Mora's thorn-punctured foot finally settled into a dull ache. His legs moved automatically, while fatigue slowly drugged him into a rhythmic trance. His eyes, through slitted lids, were fixed on the bobbing white shirt a few yards ahead. The sun rose in its long arc, then began a slow slide down the western sky. No breeze fanned them. The heat built in the low desert until every breath seemed to sear the mouth and throat. Their clothing dried quickly, then the merciless sun began sucking moisture from their bodies.

Now and then he swallowed a little from his two-quart canteen, but never took as much as he craved. He could have easily gulped down the remaining two or three pints without taking the spout from his lips. But the musty, tepid river water was more precious than liquid gold. It had to last an indefinite time. To run out of water here was to die. He hoped Quanto knew this area and was headed toward the next stream or *tinaja*. What irony — to survive snakebite and Apache knives and bullets, only to die an agonizing death of thirst.

When he next looked up, the wrinkled, gray-green mountains were perceptibly closer, but still miles away. If he was oriented correctly, those were the Sierrita Mountains. It seemed every large or small hump or ridge of desert hills in the territory had a name. He recalled the parable of the rich man in hell looking across the great chasm to heaven, begging in vain for the poor man to dip his finger into water to cool his tongue. An apt image of his own situa-

47

tion, he thought, except that he still had hopes of reaching the cooler heights of heaven in the mountains. When he did, he would part ways with Quanto, then correct his own course for Tucson. He uttered a quick prayer to St. Francis to aid him.

For now he must concentrate on conserving energy. Even though an older man required less fuel than a younger one, his strength had nearly run out. He felt disconnected from his feet and stumbled often. He was becoming lightheaded, and his eyes refused to focus on the distant mountains. Contorted arms of nearby saguaro cactus seemed to reach out for him. Then everything tilted crazily in his vision and the sandy earth came up to smack him in the side of the face.

CHAPTER THREE

Mora woke to the blessed relief of water on his face and neck, soaking his hair.

Suddenly embarrassed, he struggled to sit up, but Quanto gently pressed a hand to his chest, and he lay back in the shade of the mesquite.

"Don't waste it," Mora muttered.

As if the Indian understood, he stopped dribbling water. Mora felt the cooling effect of the moisture evaporating quickly in the dry heat. Quanto put the spout of the canteen to Mora's lips and allowed him to drink a little. The gamey water was heaven, and Mora grabbed for the canteen to tilt it up. But Quanto pulled it away, rocking back on his heels and watching.

Mora had a dull headache, but suffered more from pangs of embarrassment for needing this Indian to tend him again. He squinted at Quanto who hunkered to one side, patiently watching and waiting, an inscrutable expression on his bronzed features.

Mora closed his eyes, thinking the Indian resembled some red sandstone statue, immune to heat and thirst, as enduring as the ageless desert. Nature had designed him perfectly for this environment.

Daniel Mora, on the other hand, was from a race and culture alien to the desert and could easily be destroyed by it. It wasn't just the cool coastal mist of San Francisco he'd fled when he came east into the Arizona Territory. He would have gladly stayed in California, but for the humiliation and hardship he'd caused his family. He had hoped the desert would provide solace, a balm for his bruised spirit. But that had been two years ago, and still he'd found little peace. With the passage of time, his mind generally suppressed bad memories, retaining many of the good. But, whenever he was weak or tired, the horror of it came rushing back in all its painful frustration. Even now, as he tried to relax and recover from the humiliation of fainting from exhaustion and dehydration, the memory goaded him.

He'd been a mid-level supervisor in the General Land Office, part of the United States Department of the Interior. He'd discovered that his regional director, a man appointed by President Grant, was selling off wholesale lots of California redwoods for his own profit. Mora had patiently gathered evidence over a period of weeks, and reported the man to Washington. The Secretary of the Interior, one of Grant's so-called "Ohio gang", had tried to suppress the information. But it had reached the newspapers and a scandal ensued. The illegal logging of public lands was halted. Under pressure from Congress, the regional director was fired, prosecuted, and sentenced to prison.

Instead of being praised as a good public servant, Mora had been ostracized by his supervisors. His life was made miserable by constant harassments and official admonishments, supposedly for sloppy work. But he resisted pressure to resign. He was finally fired for insubordination when he attempted to defend himself against false accusations — fired within three years of retirement, without a pension. He'd sought solace from his wife and grown children as he cast about for some kind of job. But no comfort or understanding was forthcoming. His wife, Carrie, had wailed that he had no thought for his family's welfare, that he should have kept his mouth shut. According to her,

Mora had been a fool for doing what he considered his duty, had brought down disgrace and poverty on both of them as a result of his honesty. Even though their frame house was paid for and the bills were few, she acted as if she would have to go begging. He'd finally found a part-time job as a night watchman on the docks, but it paid little. His wife had taken a job cleaning houses of the Nob Hill wealthy. She and a grown son and daughter closed ranks and turned their backs on Daniel as if he'd ceased to exist. When Carrie deigned to address him, it was only to ridicule or find fault. At first he was treated as a fool, then a pariah.

He shrank within himself, saying little, and endured it for a year. He'd even applied for another government job, this time as a clerk with the U.S. Customs Service, mainly to qualify for retirement. But he was turned down, and later discovered he'd been blacklisted by all federal agencies. He had no recourse, since Civil Service protection laws — to replace the old spoils system — were only beginning to be discussed in Washington.

Finally he'd left it all behind. Quietly, at night, he boarded a train for Los Angeles, then a stagecoach east to Yuma. There he'd used the last of his funds to outfit himself with a burro and a grubstake, and struck off north along the Colorado River, living alone, prospecting, finding barely enough gold to buy a few staples. At first he had feared the harsh wilderness, sleeping in the open with scorpions, tarantulas, sidewinders. Leery of Indians of any tribe, he carried a loaded rifle, traveling mostly at night in the searing deserts and sleeping by day in the rugged mountains. When he finally toughened up to the rigors of his new surroundings, he had time — lots of time — to ponder other things. And loneliness crept in.

"Mora!"

He opened his eyes. The shadows had lengthened; he must have dozed. Quanto was bending over him, black eyes solicitous. "Yeah."

"¡Vámonos!"

The Indian assisted him to his feet, and handed him the carbine. Again, they started toward the mountain range.

To keep himself going until they reached the mountains, Mora continued to sip water from his canteen. No sense conserving; he'd prefer to die later of thirst, rather than sooner.

The sun finally dropped behind the mountains, leaving welcome shade. The tireless Tarahumara continued to lead. The unseen sun streaked the overhead blue with red and gold in the long summer evening. At last they reached and began to ascend the rocky slopes of the Sierritas.

Mora drained his canteen, recalling he hadn't noticed the Indian taking a drink in the past two hours. The climb took its toll on Mora's tired legs and laboring lungs, and he stopped frequently to let the muscle ache subside while he breathed heavily.

As twilight deepened, they'd ascended a third of the scarred face of the mountain. Quanto reached and entered a huge cleft in the rock, part cave, part vertical fissure. Heavier, cooler mountain air from higher up had begun its downhill slide to replace the lighter, heated air of the desert floor. This slight movement of wind fanned Mora's face and brought the smell of dampness and mold from within the crevice.

Several yards inside, they reached the apex of the cleft under an overhanging rock and found a tiny spring trickling over moss-covered rocks.

Quanto gestured for Mora to drink. Having filtered through tons of rock, the water was pure and sweet. Mora drank his fill, then stood and nodded approvingly. Quanto drank, then filled both canteens. The shadows of night were filling the hollows.

Mora was weak from hunger, but there would be no food this night, unless Quanto could magically produce more jerky from his pockets. It was his knowledge of this spring that had provided succor. Tomorrow would take care of itself.

They moved out to the flat rock at the edge of the cleft and lay down to rest. Mora placed his Marlin at his side, and Quanto still had the Apache's Colt .36 with five shots remaining. In this remote location, they should be safe enough. Yet, any roaming Apaches would surely know of this spring as well. Mora lay down and exhaustion took him within five minutes.

When he woke, stiff and sore, only a dim gray light was filtering into their shelter. Quanto still slept. Mora rose quietly, took his carbine, and padded outside, carefully climbing up where he could see down the long slope of the mountain that was covered with manzanita, scattered junipers, and dozens of plants he couldn't identify. The sky above the horizon brightened by the minute. As he watched, miles of brushy desert he'd painfully traversed turned to a lighter gray. He took a good swig from his canteen and savored the stillness.

Forty yards away, a slight movement caught his eye. When he focused in that direction, he saw nothing. Then it came again — a rabbit, hopping in and out of the brush, stopping here and there to nibble.

Mora carefully brought up the carbine. With slow, deliberate motions he worked the lever and raised the curved butt plate to his shoulder. The *crack* of the Marlin echoed off the rocky hillside.

As the sun cleared the horizon, Mora and Quanto hunkered by a small cooking fire, devouring succulent roasted rabbit — the first meal they'd eaten in more than two days. Yet, even the big jack rabbit failed to provide enough for two grown men. When they'd sucked the last of the bones and chewed every bit of gristle, Mora licked his fingers, realizing he was still hungry. But it was enough to fuel his body for more walking. Maybe they could bag additional game along the foothills.

Mora stood up and took another long drink from his canteen. He wasn't as familiar with this part of the territory, so had no idea where the next potable water might be. He carried a general map of the area in his head, and knew that Tucson lay north by east from where they stood. He was reluctant to abandon the spring Quanto had led them to, and wished for several more canteens to fill. But they had nothing to fashion another container.

How to tell Quanto that his services were no longer needed? He tried by gesture, but the Indian emphatically shook his head, then pointed to himself and Mora, and thrust a hand in the direction of Tucson. His meaning was clear.

"Well . . . if you have nothing better to do today. . . ." Mora walked back to the cool alcove and filled his canteen at the moss-covered spring. Quanto did the same and then kicked dirt on the embers of their fire.

Mora grinned. He was used to speaking to his burro, who likely understood, but couldn't respond in words. So he expected no reply when he said: "Tucson or Bust!" He stepped off toward that village, some thirty miles away.

For the first hour, until his muscles were thoroughly warmed and the energy provided by breakfast took hold, Mora walked with pain and soreness. But he paid little attention, knowing it would pass.

They traveled the foothills, descending into the flat desert only when the washes or tumbled boulders made the going tough.

That evening, Mora, with his excellent

shooting eye, bagged another rabbit — robbing some soaring hawk or owl of a meal, he remarked to Quanto. He continued talking to the Indian, never knowing how much or how little the Tarahumara understood.

Supper was a repeat of breakfast, and just as delicious in spite of having no salt, or bread, or vegetables. But this wasn't about taste or proper nourishment — it was about renewing their strength.

Since they were out in the open that night, they alternated standing guard. There were no alarms. Except for the unseen life and death struggles among nocturnal hunters and the hunted, the night was devoid of danger to humans.

Next morning the two men struck out in a more easterly direction, leaving the mountain chain behind. Their water gave out, but Mora used his belt knife to slice out pulpy chunks of barrel cactus. They squeezed the juice into their mouths. Not palatable, but at least wet and non-poisonous.

In late afternoon, they reached the San Xavier del Bac mission. While Quanto waited patiently in a pew, Mora again gave thanks at a shrine of St. Francis. Mora had no idea what religious beliefs the Indian might hold. But Quanto apparently respected this old church as a place of special meaning, remaining respectfully out of the way. Mora did notice him gazing warily at two Yaqui Indians who came in and knelt at the altar rail.

Outside, Mora and Quanto filled their canteens from a pump and, in the gathering dusk, started the last leg of their journey. By full dark, they reached the scattered hovels and adobe buildings of Tucson.

Lacking money, Mora stopped at the nearest saloon to ask directions while Quanto remained discreetly outside in the dark. He did the same when they reached the stage office several blocks away.

"Sumpin' I can do for you?" A stocky agent in vest and white shirt came to the counter.

Mora took a deep breath. The man exuded hostility. "When's the next westbound stage?"

The agent removed the stub of an unlighted cigar from his mouth. "Ten in the morning, if he's on schedule."

"What's the fare to Sand Tank station?"

"Twelve dollars."

Mora hesitated, embarrassed to frame the next question. "I'm a little short of cash. Can I muck out your stables for a ticket?"

"Figured you for a tramp when you come in here," the agent said, glancing at the trail-worn clothes and scuffed moccasins. He started to say something else, but caught himself as his gaze rested on the carbine Mora carried.

Mora felt his cheeks burning under the salt and pepper stubble. It was just this sort of treatment he'd left civilization to escape. He gave it one last try. "No odd jobs I could do for a bite to eat and a ticket?"

"Well, you might just be in luck. My stable hand got drunk and fell off his horse last night. Broke his arm. You can have the job. Pitchforks and shovels just inside the barn door. A twelve-dollar ticket's worth more than one night's work, but, if you'll oil all the harness hanging in the tack room, it's a deal." He turned away toward his desk. "By the way, if you need a place to sleep, you can bed down in an empty stall when you get done. But, no smokin', mind you. Don't want the place burned down."

"Thanks. You got a deal. Would a really good job buy me one extra ticket?"

"Don't push your luck." The agent glanced around. Mora stood alone in the office. "Somebody else goin'?"

"Maybe."

"The job ain't worth that much, and the company don't like me passin' out free tickets." He paused. "Tell you what . . . I'll give you an extra silver dollar outta my own pocket if the job's done right and you fork down some hay into them stalls, and pour a little grain into the feed boxes. There's a big pile for the old straw and manure out back."

Mora nodded, knowing he was doing the man a favor. The agent would have had to do the dirty work himself, since it was unlikely another stable hand could be hired before the next stage came in. And who knew when one of the bosses might show up and find the stables a mess? Mora was aware the Texas and California Stage Company ran a tight operation. They had to be efficient to remain in business, since their coaches would inevitably lose this route to the Southern Pacific that had already built its line east as far as Yuma.

As Mora turned to leave, satisfied he'd done the best he could, he paused by the pot-bellied stove and touched the blackened coffee pot. Still warm.

"Go ahead and help yourself," the agent said. "I'll be throwin' it out when I close up shortly." He paused. "Besides, you look like you could use sumpin' to perk you up."

Mora didn't need a second invitation. It had been weeks since he'd had a cup of coffee. He filled a tin cup and swigged down the bitter, lukewarm brew, getting a mouthful of grounds in the process. Then he poured the dregs of the pot into the nearly empty canteen, and left.

In the shadows at the corner of the adobe building, he handed the canteen to Quanto and pointed him toward the stables. The Indian took a gulp of the coffee and made a wry face. Mora grinned in the semidarkness; he'd finally gotten a reaction of some kind from his impassive traveling companion. But then Quanto decided the stuff wasn't too bad and drained the canteen.

"Reckon you did OK," the station agent said, hands on hips and looking around at the clean stalls. Early sunlight was lancing through gaps in the board wall. "You ain't lookin' for permanent work, by any chance?"

"No, thanks. Took us a good part of the night to finish cleaning and oiling all that harness."

"Well, here's the silver dollar I promised you. Come on into the office and I'll get that ticket." He glanced at Quanto. "Hope he ain't Apache."

"Tarahumara."

"What? Oh, that tribe down in Mexico?"

"Yeah." He offered no further explanation.

They entered the office and the agent made out the ticket to Sand Tank station and handed it to Mora. "Probably better if your friend stays outside. He ain't too good for my business."

Mora walked Quanto out onto the wooden porch, and indicated by sign for him to stay there.

A big man, dressed in overalls, tan shirt, and sweat-stained hat, with leather gloves protruding from a hip pocket, passed them and entered the office.

"This here's my hostler, Bill Butler," the agent said when Mora reëntered the room. "I'm goin' over to the Shoo Fly Restaurant for breakfast. He's in charge until I get back."

On impulse, Mora thrust out the silver dollar. "Since the Indian probably isn't welcome over there, would you mind buying us something to eat and bringing it back?"

"OK." The agent took the money and left.

By the regulator on the back wall, it was only eight-fifteen. They had at least a two-hour wait for the stage.

"You know if the westbound stage is on time?"

Butler was busy lighting a cigar. "Don't have no notion. The Injuns cut the wire

63

through Apache Pass every time ya turn around, so we don't get a telegraph message if it's delayed." He blew a cloud of smoke at the ceiling.

Mora went back outside and the two men sat on the edge of the porch.

Two matronly women in colorful shawls sauntered past. A white man rode by on horseback, kicking up dust. A horse pulling a light buggy swung up to the hitching rack and a young man in a white shirt and vest jumped down. He dragged a canvas sack, stenciled **U.S. Mail,** from behind the seat and, slinging it over his shoulder, entered the office. A minute later, he hurried back out, perspiring in the morning heat, and climbed into the buggy, unwrapping the lines and slapping them over the back of the sorrel.

Already full of self-importance and trying to impress his boss, Mora thought. *How like him I was thirty years ago. Look at me now . . . an old desert rat reduced to mucking out stables for food and stage fare.* In spite of the fact that he'd slept well on the clean-smelling, soft bed of hay, he was feeling sorry for himself. That usually happened only when fatigue made his problems seem insurmountable. He could have stayed home and been miserable. He hadn't had to abandon his former life and become a hermit in this god-forsaken country to remain unhappy. Yet, he knew, deep down, the desert solitude had been good for him. This brief touch with civilization was what had soured his outlook, causing him to feel cheap again in the world of human commerce.

"Quanto, I wish you and I could talk. Might find out why the hell you're tagging along." He shook his head. "Maybe I don't really want to know. My faith in human nature couldn't stand another jolt. I'd just as soon think of you as my altruistic guardian angel."

A half hour later, the station agent returned with two plates of fried ham and biscuits. The two men ate like starving wolves. Then Mora returned the plates to the restaurant, and the two men helped themselves to coffee inside the office.

At twenty past ten, the stage rolled in, trace chains rattling, a cloud of dust boiling up behind it.

"Whoa! Whoa!" The driver set the foot brake and climbed down, tossing the reins to the hostler, Bill Butler, while a Mexican boy jumped to unhitch the tired team.

Two men alighted and handed down two women. One of the well-dressed couples, apparently husband and wife, were greeted by a man in a buckboard and driven away.

Overhearing part of the conversation of the other two, Mora guessed they were casual acquaintances — through passengers who'd alighted to stretch their legs during the brief stop.

Twenty minutes later, a fresh team was hitched and the driver was calling for everyone to board. Mora handed the driver his ticket. "My friend doesn't have a ticket. I'm short of cash, but if you'll take us both to Sand Tank Station, I'll get the money there."

The driver set down his tin cup and brushed his sweeping mustache with the back of his hand. He looked Mora up and down, and then glanced at Quanto standing behind him. "We ain't in the business of haulin' passengers for free . . . especially redskins."

"Lila Strunk, the stationkeeper at Sand Tank, is a good friend of mine. She'll lend me the fare."

"You know Lila?" The driver hesitated.

The shotgun guard was stowing the mail sack in the boot and the Mexican boy held the stage door open for the woman passenger to reboard.

"I've known her a while. She's good for

the money," Mora insisted.

"Hell, lots of people know Lila Strunk. Don't matter about the fare. I got a refined white lady in that coach. I ain't exposin' her to no dirty savage."

"He could ride up top."

The driver strode toward the door, pulling on his calfskin gloves. He paused and turned back. "Didn't you hear me right, mister? I said *no!*"

CHAPTER FOUR

"Driver, here's fifteen dollars. That should cover this man's fare, and you can keep the change. He'll be my guest."

A well-dressed man with flaring, tawny mustache and thick blond hair stepped forward, holding his hat in one hand. For the first time, Mora took note of the male passenger who'd debarked from the stage and evidently overheard the conversation. He was lean, of middle height, dressed in a gray suit. Probably a youngish forty, Mora guessed.

"Pardon the intrusion," the stranger said, his blue eyes darting from Mora to Quanto. "Please accept my offer. No strings attached, as you Americans say. It's been a long, dusty trip and I'd be glad for your company. Any stories you could tell to entertain me would more than repay me." The man spoke with a British accent.

"Why, thank you. I accept with pleasure."

Here was help from an unexpected source. "I'm Daniel Mora, and this is my friend, Quanto. He's of the Tarahumara people in Mexico."

"I told you I ain't haulin' no Injuns!" the driver snapped. "He'd upset the lady passenger."

"What's your name, sir?" the Englishman asked the driver. "I'm reporting you to the Texas and California Stage Company for refusing paying passengers on a run that's half empty."

The driver clenched his jaw and said nothing. Finally he grunted, snatched the sawbuck and the five dollar gold piece, and hitched up his gun belt. "I'm holdin' you responsible for him till he gets off at Sand Tank."

The Englishman stepped up to Mora. "Lyle Coopersmith," he said, holding out his hand. "Happy to make your acquaintance."

"The pleasure is mine." Mora was at a loss for more words, but Coopersmith continued.

"I believe we're about to depart. We'll talk on the way."

The driver and guard were already in their seats when the four passengers climbed aboard, Quanto last. As the Indian cleared the doorway, the driver cracked his whip. *"Hyah!"* The fresh team jumped ahead as one, and the Mexican boy holding the door sprang out of the way of the rear wheel, yelling at the driver in Spanish.

Quanto was thrown into the lap of the woman passenger.

"Sorry, ma'am," Mora said, helping the Indian to the seat facing the woman and Coopersmith. "Guess the driver was in a hurry to get going."

"Irritated with me, I'd say," Coopersmith said, reaching to close the door that was swinging loose. The team was already at a dead run, and dust billowed through the open windows. Within 100 yards, the driver reined the team back to a walk.

The dour-looking woman didn't acknowledge the apology as she busied herself reshaping the crushed hat on her lap. She had gray hair and wore a black and lavender high-necked dress, in defiance of the heat. *With that tightly laced corset, she probably has the endurance of a cavalry sergeant,* Mora thought. He wondered how she felt about sharing the coach with three men — two of them very dirty, one of whom was an Indian. At least she was seated next to the courteous and clean Lyle Coopersmith in case she was worried the two new men

70

might get rowdy. Mora wondered where the older woman, traveling alone, could be headed in this wilderness. Wherever it was, she was not about to enlighten them as she arranged herself more comfortably, planted her feet on her small carpetbag, and closed her eyes. The coach was only lightly rocking now on the rutted road. At the pace they'd started in this heat, the horses wouldn't have made the next swing station.

"Mora . . . Mora," the Britisher said thoughtfully, fixing him with a frank gaze. "Sounds as if you must be of Italian descent."

"No. Mora and Muir are actually old Irish words for the sea. Some ancestor was evidently a seafaring man, perhaps a fisherman."

"I see. When surnames were evolving, one or more of my forebears apparently built barrels. Each of us has come from somewhere . . . including him." He nodded toward Quanto.

"Mister Coopersmith, by any chance, do you speak Spanish?" Mora asked.

"Definitely not. One of several gaps in my education."

"I'll have to wait a little longer, then, to find a translator so Quanto and I can speak to each other."

The Britisher looked surprised. "You're traveling together, yet you can't communicate?"

"Oh, we can communicate on a rather basic level. We just can't do it in words."

"Intriguing. Would you like to tell me more?"

"I prospect for gold in this vast territory," Mora said. "I'd gone down across the border into the Sierra Madre to try my luck . . . ," and he proceeded to recount his accident, his meeting with Quanto, and all that had transpired since.

Coopersmith did not interrupt as the miles rolled past under their rocking coach and the woman either slept or ignored them with her eyes closed.

"Absolutely amazing!" he breathed when the tale was brought current. "All of that in a fortnight! Even stories brought back by British soldiers from Afghanistan can't top that." He reached into his coat pocket and produced a notebook and pencil. "Do you mind if I jot a few notes? I'm gathering information for a book on the American West."

Mora was suddenly apprehensive. Had he sought refuge and anonymity in the desert only to wind up telling his story to a reporter? "Do you write for a newspaper or magazine?"

"No. I'm doing this on my own. Actually the British ministry sent me to report on the construction of the Southern Pacific Railroad extending east from California and soon to be crossing this desert."

"You Brits had railroads before we did. Why do you need a report on this one?"

"Of course we have railroads at home and in a few places around the world, but it's my job to report the details of construction, supply, the fending off of hostile natives, and the like. The ministry thinks this might help save the British government a few pounds and worries when they begin construction in some of our remote desert colonies. I'm not interested in how it's being financed, or by whom. The competition between wealthy, unscrupulous American financiers, making deals, bluffing and buying each other out, does not apply in England. Frankly that sort of thing bores me, anyway. I'd rather be in the field inspecting the construction of the road and talking with civil engineers, laborers, track bosses, and the like. As long as I do my work properly and turn in a timely report, my chief doesn't care that I'll be gathering material for my own book." He set the notebook in his lap, extracted a large, blue bandanna from his inside coat pocket, and mopped his face and neck. "Beastly hot. Did I say it was hot in India? This is the next thing to Hades, but . . . well, when I volunteered for this assignment, I told them heat didn't bother me. Yet I got the job mainly because I work cheap." He smiled.

"So this book you're writing," Mora said, bringing him back on track, "is about what exactly?"

"I'll decide when I find it," he said simply. "No preconceived notions. Tales such as yours . . . and others. The American West is vast, and I could write volumes on what I see and experience here. But I'll have to cram it all into one book. The common Englishman has an abiding interest in the American West. If my prose is compelling, this book will sell well back home."

At one o'clock they pulled into Stanwyck station. "Thirty minute stop for lunch!" the driver called, climbing down. He and the shotgun guard strolled off toward the corral to have a smoke while the hostler unhitched the team.

The four passengers got out to stretch and check the bill of fare. An odor of rancid grease assaulted Mora's nose as they entered the low, adobe building with a packed dirt floor. He and Coopersmith exchanged glances. "Food's included in the fare," the Englishman said. "Can't be finicky, or we go hungry."

"Reckon that's how she keeps her figure?" Mora grinned, jerking his head toward the woman passenger who'd entered the room, sniffed, then just as quickly retreated outside and headed for the privy.

"Whalebone probably has a lot to do with it," Coopersmith said with a twinkle in his hazel eyes.

Mora was beginning to like this man.

The lean stationkeeper sported lanky black hair and a hangdog look as he entered from the adjacent kitchen. Without bothering to brush the dead flies from the wooden table, he set down a tray, four tin plates, a small iron pot of *frijoles,* a plate of curled-up fatback, and something that resembled discs of fried dough. "Either dry flapjacks or fat tortillas," Mora commented when the man departed.

The stationkeeper returned with a tin pitcher and cups.

Quanto, Mora, and Coopersmith sat on the benches to eat. Mora poured and gulped down a cupful of the weak tea before he felt the grit between his teeth. "Ugh! Could've taken some of the desert out of this."

Coopersmith set down his own cup. "A little sand for your craw," he remarked, clearing his throat.

Quanto ate silently. But the way he put away the food showed how hungry he was. Mora guessed the Indian ate a lot when he could get it and stoically fasted when times were lean. The rhythms of life were probably all the same to him, for he seemed to take things as they came. Yet, Quanto might not have these characteristics at all. The Tarahumara couldn't speak English and showed little emotion, which effectively concealed his innermost thoughts.

While they were finishing, the woman came into the room and helped herself to a long drink of the gritty tea, then departed without saying a word. Mora watched her through the glassless window as she strolled around behind the station. He noticed her glancing about as if to be sure she was alone, then she removed a small silver flask from her handbag, uncapped it, and tipped it up.

Mora nudged the Englishman and pointed.

"That's one way to get through the day," Coopersmith commented.

"Maybe it's our company," Mora said. "Last time I bathed was in a river, fully dressed. And it's been two weeks since I stood next to a razor."

A team of frisky mules pulled the coach thirty miles to the next swing station where a six-horse hitch replaced them.

During the long afternoon while the woman dozed and Quanto stared out the window at the passing desert, Mora and Coopersmith talked quietly. Mora found himself trusting this man and gradually let slip details of his own past — how he happened to be here.

The English writer seemed genuinely interested. He took more notes. "Just to stimulate my rusty memory," he said. "You can rest easy. I won't use your name in anything I write."

After entertaining his own thoughts for months on end, Mora felt a genuine relief to be able to converse with an intelligent man. He'd almost forgotten such people inhabited the world. He instinctively trusted this man.

As the hours wore on, heat and fatigue took their toll, and the conversation flagged.

It was past ten o'clock that night when they pulled into Maricopa Wells, the largest stage stop between Tucson and San Diego. The driver told them it was one of the many abandoned Butterfield stage line stations resurrected after the war. The improvements were obvious. The presence of plentiful water from spring-fed ponds had allowed the owner to expand. The complex consisted of a dozen stone outbuildings, a store and blacksmith shop, a large corral and stable, a herd of cattle and sheep, along with crops and hay fields. Considerable trade was carried on with the Maricopa Indians as well as with passing freighters and stage passengers.

The woman passenger departed, her traveling bag carried away by a well-dressed older man.

The trio of remaining passengers lingered for an hour, while the driver and guard were switched, as well as the team.

"Wouldn't mind spending a little more time here," Coopersmith said as the three men sat down at a dining table.

"An oasis in the desert," Mora concurred, eyeing the beefsteak and boiled corn that was set in front of them. Thick adobe walls and wooden floors insulated the room from the outside night. He dug into his food, glancing at the long bar that stretched across one end of the spacious dining room. It was backed by rows of champagne and whiskey bottles. From somewhere in an adjoining office he could hear the rattle of a telegraph key.

"The Southern Pacific will likely reach this station by early next year," Coopersmith said.

"Really?" Mora had been out of touch with human events for many weeks.

"Construction's been interrupted for a few months at Yuma, and most of the crew laid off for now, but I'll still get a story from the track bosses." He looked around the spacious room at the men coming and going. "You know, I wouldn't be surprised if Maricopa Wells makes a bid to be the territorial capital. Frankly, I think it's going to be Prescott. Better climate, more centrally located. Although the Old Pueblo at Tucson has a claim, as well as that growing, upstart town, just north of here, named Phoenix."

Coopersmith had obviously done his research before coming to America. In spite of the fact that he was surrounded by evidence of advancing white civilization and its amenities, Mora found his thoughts drifting to the windswept mesas, the silence of the long desert spaces. Even as a young man he'd had a natural affinity for solitude. Only when he'd finally been forced to leave California had he found what his nature craved. As much as he was thankful for the company of Coopersmith and the life-saving efforts of Quanto, he missed the blessed silence and beauty of the desert.

"Might I inquire what your plans are after you reach Sand Tank?" Coopersmith asked.

"Try to get a stake from Lila Strunk, the stationkeeper, and go back to prospecting."

"What about your friend, here?" He nodded toward Quanto.

"Lila can speak Spanish. I'll ask her to explain that he needs to go back to his people, since I'm basically a loner."

The Englishman nodded, looking thoughtful. "Your bandoleer has a lot of gaps in it," he observed. "This store would be a good place to stock up on cartridges. Ammunition of all kinds here."

"I have no money, and I can't take yours."

"Consider it an investment. What about your Indian friend's revolver?"

"He's got only five shots in it. We didn't stop to ask that Apache for more."

"Then it'll be my pleasure to make sure both of you are well supplied."

Mora was uneasy with this, but didn't know how to refuse gracefully.

"We already owe you for Quanto's stage fare."

Coopersmith waved off the objection. "Let's go take a look."

The men got up and started into an adjoining room that held a dry-goods store.

When they reported back to the stage with plenty of fresh cartridges, they discovered the back axle of the Concord had split. The coach was on a jack and the rear wheels already removed. It would be several hours before a replacement could be made in the wagon shop. The three men were shown to a bunkhouse where they stretched out for some welcome sleep uninterrupted by the bouncing coach. Mora was thankful that none of the employees of this station showed any intolerance of his Indian companion. Maricopa Wells was constantly a-swarm with Mexicans, Indians, whites, and mixed-bloods of all kinds. Business was booming and only hostile Indians were unwelcome.

It was well past sunup before the repaired coach, pulled by a fresh six-horse hitch, was ready to roll west out of Maricopa Wells.

A lean, leathery man, threw a small grip into the rear boot and joined the three men inside the coach. "Howdy, gents," the newcomer said. "Dane Aston." He shook hands with the two white men and nodded at the Indian. "I'm a driver for this line. But I'm a passenger to Yuma this trip."

"How far to Sand Tank station?" Mora asked.

"Thirty-five miles."

"Any threat of Apaches from here on?" Coopersmith asked, fingering the bird's-head grip of a nickel-plated Colt Lightning that was holstered, butt-forward, at his belt. The Englishman had changed into worn Levi's and a light cotton shirt. The gray suit had disappeared into his luggage.

Aston laughed shortly. "Are there thorns on a cactus? Hell, yes, they're a threat! It'll be a hundred years before those red devils are under control or killed off. We sure ain't gonna make peace with them. They're fightin' to hang onto this desert like it was prime real estate." He turned to look out the window. "Matter of fact, I'll show you something up ahead about a mile or so. It ain't just the whites the Apache been warrin' with." He was silent for several minutes, scanning the terrain. "There, we're coming up to it now. Take a look at that." He pointed.

Looming up on the side of the hill, in bold outline against the blue sky, stood a rude cross upon which hung a dried body.

"About two year ago, the Maricopas crucified that Apache."

The dried arms and legs were fastened with cords and the head hung forward, a few tufts of long hair still blowing about the withered face. Mora felt a cold chill run up his sweaty back at the grim sight.

"The Maricopas don't profess the Christian faith," Aston continued, "but this much they learned from the missionaries . . . that crucifixion was a type of torture practiced by the whites."

"I've read that scalping was another," Coopersmith said in an awed tone.

CHAPTER FIVE

The barbaric sight of the crucified mummy put a damper on conversation, and the white men joined Quanto in entertaining their own thoughts while the miles unwound behind the swaying coach.

The stage had no escort, but driver and shotgun messenger, plus the four male passengers, were all armed. Apaches would pay dearly for any attack.

Glancing at Quanto's impassive face, Mora wondered if the Indian was even thinking about his tribe's ancient nemesis. Not likely. Quanto fought fire with fire. He'd used their own stealthy tactics to waylay the Apache in the mission church. His relaxed demeanor, and half-closed eyes were deceiving. The Indian would not be caught unaware.

Mora sighed and settled back against the dark leather seat. Even though he enjoyed his conversation with Coopersmith, it was a relief to be silent for a time. Silence fostered thought. Talking fatigued him, and he'd run his mouth too much the past few days. He envied Quanto who had two reasons to remain quiet — the obvious barrier of language and the social barrier between him and the three white men.

More and more, as he pursued the solitary life in this vast, arid country, Mora relaxed into himself, realizing this was apparently the life that suited his natural tendencies. He couldn't imagine how he'd functioned in a bureaucracy, or in the hectic world of family life. It wasn't that he was selfish or self-centered. He liked many people, and loved his family. But humans could best be appreciated *en masse,* from a distance. Mankind was loveable; individuals often were not. Society would probably be more peaceful if there were more hermits, he reflected. But he just as quickly realized that there would then be fewer children and no parents to rear them, probably fewer inventions, like the steam engine and photography, which had built on previous discoveries. He'd read that primitive man, who'd lived in small, societal groups, had been just as war-like as modern man, but their clashes were not as large. Human nature had not changed — only the capacity for killing.

Now massive armies marched and slaughtered each other at the behest of politicians and generals.

The thought of politicians made him squirm. Ulysses Grant was finally out of office. If that man had never been elected, Mora might still have his job and his life in California. Or, if Grant and his greedy minions had not been so corrupt — the Whiskey Ring, Secretary of War Belknap accepting bribes from an Indian trader, the stealing of funds from the sale of public timber. . . . If, if, if. . . . A man had to deal with what *was,* not with some imaginary, perfect world.

He turned to squint at the outside glare of sunshine, shucking his mind free of these morbid musings. He was done with all that, and had no second thoughts about exposing the corruption of his boss. No use raking up the painful past. The haunts of men and their problems were behind him. His life was in this wilderness now, and he'd reconciled himself to the fact that he'd die here of heart failure, old age, or the elements, or even by bullet or arrow from some hostile. Of course, he'd take normal precautions, but something was bound to get him, sooner or later.

The desert terrain was mostly level from

Maricopa Wells to Sand Tank station, and, much of the time, the driver walked the team to keep from wearing them out in the heat over the longer, thirty-five mile stretch. The coach rocked gently and Mora dozed off. In late afternoon, he awoke, perspiring, as the coach pulled into the oasis at Sand Tank station.

He climbed down, stiff-jointed, with the others, and wiped his face on his sleeve. "Thought you were going on to Yuma," he said to Coopersmith.

"Sustenance," the Britisher replied.

"Forty-minute stop for supper!" the driver called over his shoulder as he and the guard and the deadheading driver walked off by themselves.

Mora paused at the familiar sight. Chinked cottonwood logs, weathered silver gray on the outside, formed walls two feet thick. Two separate rooms were joined by a roofed dogtrot, covering a bubbling spring — the only water within miles. Mora knew that when the builders of the Butterfield Stage Line appropriated this scarce water as their own nearly thirty years before, it had infuriated the Apaches. During the war, Butterfield had abandoned the station and the Apaches had assumed their numerous raids had discouraged the white encroachers. But the building had been rebuilt in the 1870s, and the unguarded spring once more taken over for use with a stage station. Six months ago, shortly after Mora's last visit here, an Apache raid had killed Frank Strunk, the stationkeeper. Lila had survived only because she'd been tending one of their irrigated fields at the time, and hid until the raiders made off with their horses.

If there were any one place Mora could call home since he'd fled California, this was it. He followed Coopersmith and Quanto into the low-ceilinged room. The aroma of fried steak and onions rang the bells of memory. The last time he'd smelled that, Lila Strunk had been serving it.

"Have a seat, gents!" a female voice called from the open door of the other room. "Grub'll be right out!"

The voice was followed a minute later by a short, lean woman, carrying a platter of smoking meat and a bowl of steaming beans that she set on the plank table. Her brown hair was clasped at the nape of her neck with a tortoise-shell comb. She wore an apron over her calico dress.

"By heaven, Dan Mora!" She gave him a hug and kiss. "Didn't expect to see you here."

Mora felt his face flushing at this show of

88

affection. "Lost my burro, and my whole outfit," he mumbled.

"How?" She pulled away, holding his arms, a look of concern on her tanned face.

"Tell you later. But this man saved my life . . . twice."

She looked where he pointed. Quanto was already seated at the bench, ready to eat. She frowned. "An Indian?"

"Yeah. Name's Quanto. He's a Tarahumara from Mexico. That's about all I know about him since he doesn't speak English and I don't speak his language, or Spanish."

"Well, I know there are good and bad of all races, but I don't have any truck with Indians, especially since they killed Frank. But . . . if he saved your life, he can sit at my table any time." She nodded curtly at the three men, then disappeared out the door through the dogtrot to the kitchen.

Three-quarters of an hour later, the meal was finished. Coopersmith gripped Mora's hand as he started for the door. "I'd like to stay and see what happens from here on, and why that aborigine has fastened himself to you. But duty calls. With luck, I'll see you again, although chances are slim."

"Where you headed?"

"End-of-track at Yuma. Hope to discover when the Southern Pacific will resume construction."

"Soon as I get some money, I'll leave what I owe you here with Lila. Might take me a few weeks, though."

"You don't owe me anything for his fare or for the ammunition. You've given me permission to use your story in my book, and that's payment enough for me."

"I hope my story has a happy ending," Mora said, shutting the stage door after Coopersmith, who was now the sole passenger.

"The end is too far off to be considered just now!" the Englishman called over the driver's shout as the stage lurched into motion.

"That driver always gallops the team for a bit to take the edge off their feistiness," Lila Strunk said, coming up to stand beside Mora as he watched the dust cloud rolling up behind the departing stage.

A few minutes later, the stage was only a smudge of brown dirt in the distance. After the rumble of hoofs and wheels had faded and they could no longer hear the crack of the driver's whip, a sense of isolation crept in to fill the space around the station. In the silence, a light breeze rustled the leaves of giant cottonwoods nearby. Yet Mora's feeling was one of peace, rather than isolation.

"I was hoping you'd stay for a spell," Lila finally said, turning to him.

"Lila, I've got to ask for your help."

"Sure. Anything."

"I'm busted. I need a small stake to get going again."

"I've got a little money saved you can have."

"Not money. I mean an animal, some food. I know areas in the Chocolate Mountains where I can pick up some float. . . ."

"That's 'way over north of Yuma, isn't it?"

"Yeah. I can get there in a week or two, traveling mostly at night." He smiled down at her. "I'm a prospector. Time isn't my enemy."

"You're welcome to anything I have. There's a mule I put out to pasture you can take. I'll buy him cheap from the company for you. He's getting old and isn't up to pulling a stage anymore, but he's still sound of wind and limb, and I believe he'll hold up for a while longer, if you don't overwork him." She walked into the shade of the cottonwoods, letting the warm desert wind fan her flushed face. "Whew! The worst part of this job is standing over a cook stove in this heat."

"Why do you stay on here?" he asked, putting a foot on the split-log bench under the big tree.

"Where else can I go? What else can I do?"

"A woman like you has a lot to offer. You'd be a success darned near anywhere."

She gave him a disgusted look and shook her head. "I'm not some young thing you can flatter with that kind of blarney, Daniel Mora."

"You'll have to make a choice pretty soon," he said. "How long before the railroad comes through here and puts you out of business?"

"The Southern Pacific has been stalled at Yuma for a year due to lack of funds. From what I hear, Collis Huntington is getting close to rounding up the public and private money he needs to start building again. Construction will move fast when they do. I'm guessing it'll be a few months before they reach here. But I'm not sure if they'll come this way or go south on a straighter line to Tucson."

"Would they pass up this spring? Those steam engines need a lot of water."

"Dan, I just don't know." She stared off toward the low Sand Tank Mountains.

"Who's your hostler out there?" He pointed at a figure moving around the adobe corral.

"A Mex named Angel Rivera. A drifter

92

who works cheap. I don't trust him, but I had to have somebody after Frank died. Rivera dropped off the stage looking for a job at the right time. He sleeps in the stalls and I sleep with a Colt under my pillow."

"All the more reason you should quit and go to the city."

"I'll stick it out until the job ends . . . when the Southern Pacific puts the stage company off this route," she said, strong resolution in her voice.

He turned to look at this woman. Faint crow's-feet fanned out from the corners of her eyes from too much squinting into the desert glare. Her regular features had been pretty at one time, he was sure, but wind and sun had dry-tanned the skin of her face and neck to a leathery hue. Yet the blue eyes she turned on him were still bright and fresh.

"But let's not discuss my situation," she said. "I want to hear your story. What happened? What about this Indian?" She nodded toward Quanto who hunkered against the log wall, thirty yards away, sipping coffee from a tin cup. He had removed his blue cloth headband and was using it to tie his long black hair behind his head. His slightly hooded eyes stared out from a face that appeared to be carved from mahogany.

While the sun dropped toward the horizon, painting the western sky with breathtaking shades of red and gold, Mora related his tale of prospecting the Sierra Madre Mountains in Mexico, and the events since his accident. "Amazing the trouble one rattlesnake can cause," he concluded with a grin.

"Man proposes, God disposes," she said. "He sent you that Indian."

"I believe He did, but now I don't know what to do with him."

"What do you mean?"

"You have a working knowledge of Spanish, and I think he does, too. Could you question him to find out why he's trailing along with me?"

"I'll give it a try."

They moved toward Quanto, who drained his cup and stood up, flexing his legs.

"David Mora *es mi amigo,*" she began. Then, in hesitant Spanish, she politely asked Quanto about himself. Mora caught a word or two as she proceeded, then lost the thread of her speech.

Quanto apparently understood, since he answered with short sentences, pointing to himself, then to Mora.

Lila looked thoughtful, as if trying to translate the Indian's replies.

"As near as I can understand him, he says the Spirits sent you to him while he was out hunting. Once he'd saved you from the poison, he felt it was his duty to see you safely back to your own country."

"Thank him, but tell him I'm fine now and he can go home. Tell him he can have my outfit, if he can snare it out of that gorge."

She turned to Quanto and translated the message. His reply was longer than usual.

"He says he is about to be married, but he and his village are extremely poor. He told his intended bride he was coming to the United States with you. He'd helped you, so now he wants you to help him find work here."

Mora was frustrated. "Surely he knows I'm a prospector, a hermit, an outcast from white society."

She shrugged. "He thinks, because you're white, you can get him a job on the railroad. He apparently figures you're his ticket to a better life."

Mora sighed. "If he only knew. . . ."

"Even in this desert, the grass looks greener north of the border," she remarked.

"If I'd known this earlier, I could have sent him on with Coopersmith," Mora said.

"A foreigner wouldn't have much say with

a hard-nosed construction boss about hiring an Indian." She brushed back a strand of hair blowing across her face. "I've talked to some railroad men who've come through here on the stage. They'll hire Chinese and Irish before they'll put an Indian on the payroll. You can't imagine how much all Indians are feared and hated."

Mora thought for a moment. "Make sure Quanto understands he can have the few tiny nuggets and a little gold dust in a rawhide poke on my dead burro. It should be enough to get his married life started."

"Do these Indians know the value of gold?" she wondered aloud.

"Hell, Lila, this is Eighteen Seventy-Eight. You can bet all Indian tribes now know what that yellow metal will buy."

She translated. Quanto responded in Spanish.

"He thanks you, but says he'll need to work and save his money before he can go home. Apparently he's been selected by his village to help bring some cash to supplement what little they can grow and raise."

"Oh . . . damn!" Mora looked away in disgust. "I left home to get away from all this."

"If you don't mind my saying so, maybe you should think more in terms of escaping *to* something, rather than *from* something."

"I don't need a lecture from you, too, Lila," he said plaintively.

"If it weren't for this redskin, the *zopilotes* would be feasting on your carcass in the mountains or in the Tumacacori ruins." She was nothing if not truthful and practical.

"You're right. I owe him my life, twice over. But how do I repay him?"

"You might offer to take him with you."

"No. I travel alone. Besides, if he thinks I can lead him to gold, he's sadly mistaken. I've found barely enough color to keep myself going these last few months." He paused. "Why can't he stay here and work as your hostler? He helped me at the stage stable in Tucson." He failed to add that Quanto had little to do with handling the stock.

She turned to the Indian and, with many gestures, attempted to explain what she and Mora had been discussing.

He replied in a few short sentences. Mora could guess the answer even before she translated.

"He says he knows nothing about horses since he and his people have always traveled by foot." She paused and looked toward a figure moving around the adobe corral. "Besides, the stage company doesn't pay

much. That's why I'm stuck with Rivera."
After a pause, Mora said: "Let's see to that
mule."

Might as well change the subject, he
thought, since he had no ready solution to
the problem of Quanto.

She led the way to the adobe corral.
"Rivera, bring Estes over here."

A lean Mexican with stringy black hair
and a thin mustache took a lariat from the
snubbing post and shook out a loop. The
docile old mule, standing in the shade of
the stable, was roped and led to the adobe
wall.

Mora tried not to stare at Rivera. This
Mexican looked shifty-eyed — not someone
he'd care to meet in a dark alleyway. Mora
reached to look at the animal's mouth, but
jerked his hand back as the fractious old
mule snapped at him with worn, yellow
teeth. "Nice disposition," Mora remarked,
noting the scars from old galls on the mule's
hide. One eye was slightly rheumy. This
animal's best days were long past, and Mora
didn't want a beast he might have to shoot
for food before he got to Yuma.

"You don't have a burro or a horse?" he
asked.

" 'Fraid not. It's Estes, here, or shanks
mare."

"*Hmm* . . . think I'll take up your offer of a stake of money," he said. "If you can spare it."

"What have I got to spend it on out here?" she asked as they walked back toward the station.

"Is it enough to pay stage fare to Yuma *and* buy a burro and supplies?" He felt blood rising to his face and didn't look at her. Begging never came easy for him.

"Should be . . . if you're careful."

"You know I'll pay you back."

"I'm not worried about that." She gave him an easy smile. "It's an investment in the future. It's my assurance you'll be back."

"I won't take advantage of our friendship," he assured her. "I'll accept the money only on the condition that you get half of any discoveries I make. That's the standard offer."

"Agreed." He thought he noted a twinkle in her eye as she held out her hand and they shook, formally, to seal the bargain. "Now, that's settled. All we have to figure out is what to do about your friend, Quanto."

The decision was deferred. Mora and Quanto slept on the hard plank floor that night. Next day they helped Lila with various chores, chopping and splitting the scarce firewood for her cook stove, collecting dried cow chips from the irrigated pasture where a half-dozen cattle grazed.

Shortly after noon, Mora sent Quanto to help Rivera unhitch the team from the eastbound stage while he himself served the food Lila cooked for the nine passengers that crowded into the small room. In less than an hour, the stage was gone and they were washing the tin plates and cups.

"I just keep a little of this cooked grub for myself between stage runs," Lila said in answer to Mora's question. "Too hot to be cooking all the time for just myself and Rivera."

"He comes inside here to eat?"

"Now and then, but I don't let him make a habit of it. I don't want him to get the idea that I'm an easy mark."

"You think he's liable to try to rob you?"

"I wouldn't put it past him, if he gets a chance. But I keep him on his heels 'cause I don't follow a regular routine. I'm rattling around here in the middle of the night, as often as not, when I'd normally be sleeping. He can't get a fix on me."

"Does he have a gun?"

"Not that I know of. But I do. And he knows it. He carries a knife in his boot and it's like a razor, and he's good with it. Wouldn't put it past him to slit my throat if he could catch me off guard."

"Damn, Lila! You need to get rid of him. Fire him. Send him away. Get one of these stage drivers to haul him outta here."

"Then what would I do for a hostler? I can't handle the horses and the cooking and everything else by myself."

"You can't handle anything if you're dead."

CHAPTER SIX

Mora held the carbine across his knees, and let his body roll with the coach's motion as it lurched into a dry wash. He was relaxed, but alert, aware of the stony, black stare from Rivera who sat opposite him. Seated next to the Mexican was a broad-shouldered man dressed in canvas and corduroy, wearing a long-barreled Colt on his hip, and holding a Stetson in his lap. His name was Russ Tanner, a construction boss for the Southern Pacific Railroad on his way to Yuma.

Things had worked out even better than Mora could have hoped. Lila had fired Rivera that afternoon while Mora stood by with his Marlin conspicuously at hand. The hostler had given her a hard look and spat something in Spanish that made Lila flush under her tan. But she'd turned to the driver of the westbound coach and paid Rivera's fare to Yuma. The single westbound passenger was Tanner. Mora had introduced him to Quanto while they were all eating Lila's supper of fluffy flapjacks and bacon.

"Quanto saved me from Apaches. Also, cured my snakebite and kept me from dying of thirst in the desert," Mora had said. "As capable a man as you'll find. Good tracker and knows the country, too."

"Mighty handy fella to have around," Tanner remarked, sipping the scalding black coffee.

"All he wants is a chance to work for the railroad on a construction gang."

Tanner had set down his cup and looked at Mora, then at Quanto, who was eating and apparently didn't understand the conversation. "We should resume grading and laying track within a few weeks," he said. "Does he have any experience?"

"No."

"Personally I don't have anything against friendly Indians. . . . I could probably put him on the grading crew, leveling the roadbed out ahead of the track-layers."

"That would be great," Mora said. "You won't be sorry. He's a good man. A lot of stamina."

"Well, I'll be needing some men. All my laborers have drifted away since we stopped construction over a year ago. The way I

103

figure it, one Indian can't do much harm by himself. And he'd be less trouble than all those damned Irishmen who're always drinking and fighting each other."

"I can vouch for the fact that he's deadly against Apaches, too. Can I tell him he's got a job, then?"

Tanner had nodded. "Have him report to me at Yuma the last of August and I'll put him to work. The Chinese get a dollar a day. We pay white men a dollar and a half. If this Indian's as good as you say, I could probably pay him the higher wage."

Mora had hardly been able to contain his gratitude, so merely said: "Thank you, Mister Tanner. You won't regret it. The only thing . . . he doesn't speak English."

"Our chinks don't either, and they get along all right."

"He's conversant in Spanish, though."

"Good. That'll work." The construction boss wiped his mouth and got up from the table.

Lila had just entered with a coffee pot and Mora gave her the news. She'd relayed the information to Quanto in Spanish. The Tarahumara grunted in the affirmative, looking pleased. During some further three-way conversation, Mora had told Quanto he must stay at Sand Tank station for two moons and work as a hostler until he could start work for the railroad. The Indian had agreed.

Lila had looked relieved as she watched Rivera board the stage under Mora's watchful eyes. The Mexican had no luggage, but had pocketed the $10 in wages Lila had paid him.

"Don't make it so long until your next visit," Lila murmured as she held Mora's arm.

"Probably a month or so," he'd said. "I'll be back to repay you."

"You know I don't care about that. Now, get on down the road and . . . watch your back. No more accidents before I see you again."

"Help Quanto with those stage horses."

"I'll show him what to do."

Barring delays, it normally took sixteen hours to reach Yuma. The sun dipped below the horizon in a welter of red and gold, and they followed the meandering desert road along the Gila during the relative coolness of night.

Mora was tired. In spite of jarring chuckholes and the commotion of two scheduled stops to change horses at swing stations, he anticipated sagging into a corner of the coach for sleep during a good portion of the trip. But did he dare close his eyes once it grew dark? He might never open them again. The bone handle of a big knife protruded from the top of Rivera's left boot. One swift motion, a deadly thrust, and Rivera might skewer him. The Mex could then leap from the slowly moving coach and be gone into the night. And, judging from the hate in the black eyes staring at him from across the coach, Mora had no doubt that's what the Mexican had in mind.

As long as Tanner, the big, armed railroad man, was awake beside him, Mora sensed no imminent danger. Lila had warned Mora about Rivera, but added that she had him sized up as a cowardly sneak who wouldn't attack unless he had a clear advantage and was sure he could get away. No doubt Rivera harbored a grudge about being fired and would look for an opportunity to avenge himself. Mora would just have to make sure it wasn't tonight.

In spite of his resolve, Mora began to fade an hour after darkness settled in. His eyelids drooped and his head fell forward every few seconds as he lost consciousness. Time and again he jerked himself awake, only to see, by moonlight, those unblinking black eyes staring at him.

At the first swing station, Mora approached the driver who was sipping coffee from a tin cup and walking the stiffness out of his legs near the corral.

"How about I ride up top the rest of the way?"

"Already got a guard," the driver replied without turning his head. The wide brim of the Stetson kept his face in deep shadow from the moonlight.

"Another pair of eyes wouldn't hurt, and I've got my carbine. It's pretty hot and stuffy inside." Mora felt he was getting better at this begging. He couldn't admit the real reason for his request — that he feared a vengeful Mexican who was armed only with a knife.

"OK, suit yourself." The driver shrugged.

The rest of the night, Mora breathed the fresh desert air as the horses trotted and the coach bounced and rolled. He slipped off the bandoleer and lay down with his rifle, bracing his feet against the thin iron rails around the roof. The empty, moonlit desert looked as peaceful as he'd ever seen it. But he wasn't fooled by appearances. Out there, beyond his view, nocturnal creatures stalked their prey, from scorpions to lizards to sidewinders, kangaroo rats, burrowing owls, perhaps an occasional pack of wild javelinas.

The cycles of life and death continued to rotate. Neither were the five men on the moving coach, along with their six horses, immune from the peril of predators — human ones in the form of the fearsome Apaches.

Toward morning, as the driver was walking the team, Mora dozed for nearly an hour. He jerked awake and grabbed for the rail as they tilted into an arroyo, the motion exaggerated by the tall coach. He looked back. The desert shrubbery was graying and the eastern sky rosy with coming dawn. He sat up and yawned, eyes gritty from too little sleep. Another beautiful, clear day. He inhaled deeply, savoring the moment. The only sounds were the muffled thudding of hoofs, the squeaking of the coach, the faint jingle of trace chains. Even the guard was nodding, half asleep, some instinctive sense of balance keeping him from falling off the box as he leaned on the stubby, twin-barreled shotgun.

All too quickly the moment passed, the fiery eye of the sun lanced across the desert, throwing long shadows out ahead of them, the guard sat up, stretched, and reached down for a drink from his canteen. The driver slapped the lines and the team broke into a trot.

At a swing station, they changed horses and ate a breakfast of flapjacks and black-strap molasses, washed down with strong coffee. Mora made sure he kept Rivera in sight, but the Mexican, except for glaring at him, made no move in his direction.

Tanner, eyes puffy from sleep, ate in silence.

The sun was straight up when the stage rolled into Yuma.

"I'll have Quanto report to you here," Mora said as Tanner was collecting his leather grip from the boot of the stage. "Where will you be?"

"Southern Pacific office at the end of the next block. We'll open 'er up in early August." He shook Mora's hand, and crossed the street toward the hotel.

Mora came around the back of the stage and nearly bumped into Rivera. He wondered if the Mexican had heard the conversation. Lila had said he understood and spoke English, but usually chose not to stoop to using the *gringo* tongue. What was the man waiting for? He had no luggage. Mora stepped up into the shade of the roofed boardwalk in front of the stage depot and watched the greasy Mexican slouch away, eyeing the store fronts. Finally he disappeared into a saloon several doors down, and Mora breathed a sigh of relief that the hostler was at last out of sight.

He hefted his Marlin and looked around for a hotel. There wasn't much to choose from, but any kind of halfway comfortable bed would be preferable to what he'd become used to for weeks. He was reluctant to spend any of his borrowed money on such luxury, but found that civilized habits were still ingrained in him. He'd even borrowed a washtub and taken a bath in the sun-warmed spring water at the Sand Tank station. Lila had given him Frank Strunk's razor. A growth of whiskers might protect his face from the fierce sun, but beards were also hot and itchy and made him feel grimy.

He'd passed through Yuma before and the town never failed to depress him. A more desolate place for a settlement, he could hardly imagine. A westerly breeze lifted and swirled a skein of dust from the street. The wind fanning his face was not cooling; it felt like the devil had opened the door of hell. Were it not for the Colorado River flowing south into nearby Mexico, living here would've been impossible, even for the Indians. About thirty years before, the Army had established Fort Yuma on the California side of the river. From all reports, it had been an outpost of civilized living prior to the coming of the railroad, with fine food for the officers, and even an organ. It was a wonder the instrument didn't fall apart, as did wagon wheels and anything else that depended on a certain amount of moisture in the atmosphere to hold its shape.

He squinted against the glare and surveyed what there was of the town — mostly a collection of adobe and stone buildings of one story that blended into the reddish-tan earth. On a slight prominence, a block away, squatted the three-year-old territorial prison. The brown stone and adobe prison might have grown out of the flat promontory overlooking the river. With its sally port, it resembled some medieval fortress in the sands of North Africa. In spite of the heat, a slight shiver ran up Mora's back at the sight. To him, freedom was everything. He had bought his at the price of his way of life. That barred enclosure represented everything he hated. He wondered what sorts of men were incarcerated there.

The heat, reflecting off the packed dirt street, seemed to shrivel him. He turned away to look for something cool to drink. There was no shortage of saloons. He made a note to avoid the one Rivera had entered, walked on down the block, and turned the corner, finding one whose front was shaded by a wooden porch. The thick adobe walls kept the dim interior somewhat cooler. The bartender lounged in a captain's chair against the wall near a back door propped open to catch any vagrant breeze. Only three other patrons were in the place. Except for the free lunch on the end of the bar, this saloon served no food.

He leaned his carbine against the bar and pointed at the closest beer tap. The bartender swished his towel at a half dozen flies that had come in out of the heat, and drew off a foamy mug.

Mora drank it down without stopping and shoved the mug across for a refill, and asked the bartender to fill his empty canteen with water as well. The second beer was halfway finished before he paused to taste the lukewarm liquid. Not as thirst quenching as the spring water at Sand Tank station, but he was so dry, anything tasted good. He paid for a third and carried it to a table where he sat, sipping for twenty minutes, planning his next move while munching on a hunk of cheese and bread from the free lunch. The Chocolate Mountains were north of here and closer to the river than the Castle Dome. In this heat, he'd be better off staying near a source of water. Maybe he'd cross over to the fort to see if he could obtain a map of the area. His own mental map was somewhat vague.

All these small clusters of desert mountains were becoming more and more populated with miners and prospectors. In spite of the Apache threat, white men were filing claims and sinking shafts. Riches held an allure that no amount of danger could quell. The mines were more silver than gold, but prospectors were finding enough of the scarce yellow metal to keep small parties of white men coming, scattering over the desolate, rocky wastes, probing the remote cañons and outcroppings. More than two years earlier, a steamship line had established Castle Dome Landing, the first boat stop on the river above Yuma, as a jumping-off point for the nearby mines. The Landing had grown into a small town with a general store, hotel, saloon, stage agency, justice of the peace, and a smelting furnace. In truth, the chances of seeing another human in the desert and mountains east of the river were slim, Mora knew, but just the idea that there were others within a few miles of him created a feeling of being crowded.

He decided to gather supplies and strike north to the nearest clump of mountains along the Colorado. If he found nothing, he'd turn east, away from the river and probe the Castle Dome area. Gold was his objective. Silver was more plentiful, but it was bulky to transport and not as valuable. Leave that to the professional miners who could afford machinery. His was a subsistence existence; he was not seeking riches.

He drained his beer, and rose to his feet, feeling much refreshed. Back out in the sunshine, he headed for the nearest mercantile to buy a wide-brimmed, light-gray hat. A man could not go bareheaded in this fierce summer sun. He asked the clerk for the best place to obtain a burro, and was directed to a stable near the river.

"If he don't have any donkeys, you might try Fort Yuma across the river," the clerk said. "They sometimes have pack animals to sell."

"I'll be back for provisions," Mora said, glancing around at the well-stocked shelves.

He hefted his rifle and walked the several short blocks to the river. As the livery stable sign came in sight, he paused to admire the squat railroad bridge built of heavy timbers. On the far side of the Colorado, a string of boxcars and several passenger coaches were parked on a siding, baking in the sun. Mora wondered where Coopersmith might be. Too bad the Englishman had missed meeting Tanner, the construction boss.

By mid-afternoon, Mora was wilting from the effects of the heat and the three beers he'd consumed. But he was satisfied he'd made a good buy on the burro. She was a slightly undersized Jenny with soft gray fur, about four years old. She'd worked as a pack animal only twice, was docile to a load, and hell on snakes, the livery owner assured him.

"Don't have no idea how sure-footed she might be in the mountains," the man said in response to Mora's query. " 'Cepten that's pretty much inborn to these animals."

The animal nuzzled his shirt pocket, smelling for a treat, and Mora rubbed her nose. "Not yet. Maybe later."

He paid the liveryman and led the burro away by the halter rope. He glanced at the tops of the buildings in the fort across the river. The Stars and Stripes waved lazily in a westerly breeze. He saw no sign of life there, or in the streets of Yuma. Maybe the entire population was inside, seeking refuge during the hottest part of the day.

At the mercantile he carefully spent most of the money Lila had lent him, laying in a stock of dried beans, rice, salt, coffee, the minimum of pans and utensils, a coil of stout rope, a shovel, short axe, an ore hammer small enough to fit in his pocket, two one-gallon metal canteens, a blanket, a coarse canvas sack, a new pair of Levi Straus's canvas pants, green glass goggles, two blocks of matches, a feedbag for his burro in case he came across some grain, and a slightly used wooden pack saddle that resembled a small sawhorse, a heavy square of canvas that could be used for a pack cover, tent, or ground cover, also purchasing a pipe and tobacco. He bought a Bowie knife big enough to chop sticks and small enough to slice bacon, and stout enough for protection. Lila had let him keep her late husband's razor. He opted for strips of *carne seca,* dried beef jerky, since a side of bacon would melt down to lean and rind in no time.

A few Mexicans were abroad on the streets in the eighty-degree coolness of early morning. As Mora secured the pack on his burro, he felt refreshed after nine hours of solid slumber in a reasonably clean hotel bed. He secured the knot and glanced at the clear sky that promised another fair, blistering day. The inner peace he craved had been interrupted by his foray into Mexico, and its aftermath. The desert beckoned.

Trudging along with the river on his left and the grim walls of the Yuma Territorial

Prison casting a long shadow across his path from the right, he thought briefly of the hardened criminals caged there. His ex-boss would still be serving a sentence somewhere in California for theft of government property. The man's own greed and dishonesty, with the help of Mora's testimony and evidence, had put him there. Mora had never doubted he'd done the right thing, even though he'd brought down the wrath of nearly everyone on his own head. He reflected that most men had only minimal control over their own lives.

He looked back at his newly acquired burro following on the lead. Whatever his own fate was to be, she would share it. "I'll name you Kismet," he muttered. "What do you think of that?"

Her reply was a brown-eyed stare and the twitching of her long ears.

He chuckled and turned ahead toward the wilderness, when he caught sight of Rivera eyeing him from across the street.

CHAPTER SEVEN

Hugh Deraux awoke to the clanging of an iron cell door, followed by cursing in English and a chatter of excited Chinese voices.

"Damn!" he muttered, rolling over on the top bunk and opening his eyes a crack to stare at the arched, whitewashed ceiling several feet above his head. Barely daylight. The noise had shattered his dream of swimming naked in a clear, cool stream with two voluptuous women. What the hell was the racket this early? It wasn't time to get up yet. His four cellmates were also stirring, looking out through the iron grate where a swinging lantern revealed three uniformed guards dragging one of the Chinese inmates out of the cell across the passageway.

Deraux rubbed his eyes and followed their gaze. One guard held a shotgun on the prisoners while the other two hefted the thin

118

Chinaman by the arms and legs and carried him up the corridor out of sight. The guard with the gun banged the cell door shut and turned a massive key in the padlock before following.

"Why can't these damn' chinks get sick in the daytime?" Deraux muttered aloud, knowing he would not be able to recapture his erotic dream. He sat up and dangled his legs over the top edge of the three-tiered bunk. Early summer daylight was growing stronger by the minute, illuminating their cell through the grated back door that opened into the exercise yard.

"He wasn't sick. He was dead," Gilbert Gilliland said, cocking his head next to the grate in an effort to see the departing guards. "It was Sing Quong. Hanged himself, by the look of it. Still had his shirt sleeve tied around his neck. Damn' near black in the face."

"Poor bastard couldn't take any more of this place," José Vasquez sighed, lying back on his bottom bunk. "Who will be next?"

Two three-tiered bunks stood against each wall of the cell, leaving only a narrow walkway between. One of the middle bunks was empty. None of them mentioned the loss of the popular and humorous John Fleming, who'd been killed a week earlier

119

by falling rock while excavating another isolation cell in the hillside. His vacant bed gave the remaining five slightly more room in the ten-by-twelve foot cell. Fleming's death, and now the suicide of Sing Quong, across the corridor, weighed on their spirits. In the ensuing quiet, Deraux heard only intermittent coughing and snoring from the other cells, and the clanking of chains. Who next, indeed? Although they were taken out to work during the day, close confinement in the cell-block at night, with a long leg chain fastened to a ring in the stone floor, allowed for the spread of disease. Consumption had carried off three men within the past four months.

"Nobody lives forever, even on the outside," José Vasquez remarked after several seconds of silence.

"Better sooner than later," Gilliland agreed.

"Shut up that kind of talk!" snapped the whiskey voice of Three-Fingered Jack Ocano, a tough half-breed and senior convict in the group of five. "All of you can whimper and die in here if you want to, but I'm planning on getting my ass outside."

"And just how you gonna do that?" the black-haired Gilliland asked.

"I'm working on it."

"When you figure out something, let us know," Vasquez said.

Three-Fingered Jack growled something under his breath, then said: "Getting killed trying to escape beats dying by inches in here . . . damned bloody floggings for sassing a guard . . . or going crazy with the heat." He sat up on the top bunk opposite Deraux, sweat matting the black hair on his massive chest. He took his striped shirt and wiped his face and thick mustache, then rubbed a glistening sheen from his bullet-bald head.

The newest or youngest men were forced to take the lowest bunks where the stench of the slop bucket was worst. And the junior convicts got the job of emptying the bucket each day, along with any other dirty job the others shunned.

"How long you in for, Jack?"

"Life."

When the big man had been put in their cell nine months earlier, he'd made no secret of his past. Only a good lawyer hired by his family had enabled him to escape the hangman for a double murder. As it turned out, his sentence was reduced to life without parole.

"You're a lifer . . . you don't have anything to lose." Mormon Bob Heenan was serving

121

three years for polygamy. "I have only sixteen more months before I'm out."

"Will your wives be glad to see you, *compadre,* or have they moved on?" Vasquez asked, grinning. "I have a leetle *puta* in Sonora. Rita Gomez . . . ahh, just the thought of. . . ."

"Dreamers! The whole damn' bunch o' you!" Three-Fingered Jack snorted. "You'll all die in here, unless you do something about it."

Although talk of escaping was a daily topic, Hugh Deraux knew the endless plotting was more for keeping their hopes up and killing time, than for anything else. Since he still had nine long years for stage robbery stretching endlessly ahead of him, he was open to any feasible plan of escape.

"What's the work detail for today?" Deraux asked Ocano to defuse the tension and get them talking about something more immediate. He and Three-Fingered Jack Ocano were the only two of the five who were assigned to hard labor outside in the hot sun. The other three were presently detailed to the laundry, bakery, and the mattress shop.

"Probably digging that chink's grave," Ocano said. "Don't look forward to that. At least chipping the rock in that second cell

122

we're cuttin' in the hillside is far enough along that we can work in the shade part of the day."

"Reckon I'll be shaping those granite rocks to fit into the north wall," Deraux said. "I like being outdoors. Wouldn't be bad if it was winter."

"How do we get such plush details?" Ocano grimaced.

"Big Bill Braxton," Deraux reminded him shortly. The brutal guard made no secret of the fact that he was out to break the will of Ocano and Deraux, who he considered leaders and troublemakers.

"When I make my break, I'll put a stop to his career at the same time," Ocano vowed. "He's laid that ironwood club across my kidneys one too many timcs. That bent-nosed bastard won't know what hit him."

"You're serious about this break, then?" Deraux said.

"Yeah, it's gotta be. . . ." He paused at the sound of a scuffing noise in the passageway outside the cell. Climbing down from the top bunk, Ocano pressed his face to the iron grate. "Gotta be careful. A couple o' these damned screws have taken to wearing gum-soled shoes to sneak around and eavesdrop."

"Hell, they don't care what we're talking about," Heenan said. "They know it's only talk. There's no escaping this place. There's a Gatling gun on the big watchtower that can sweep the whole compound. And the guard posts on the walls are always manned with men carrying loaded Winchesters. Even if you somehow get over the walls and outside, where you going to go?"

"The river's barely a hundred yards away," Gilliland said.

"Not for me, *compadre*," the handsome Vasquez demurred. "Makes me shiver to think of being sucked down in a whirlpool and suffocated in that brown water. How many of you even know how to swim?" he asked.

There was a hesitation. "I could probably manage if it isn't too swift," Gilliland said.

"I've seen it up close, and even bathed in the eddies. There's a helluva current," Deraux said. "Besides, the river's the first place they'd look."

"We could go east of here, up along the Gila," Gilliland said.

"This time o' year, the Gila would be as dry as your scaly scalp," Heenan said. "Possibly a scummy pool here and yonder, but the main road follows the Gila. Not safe."

"North, then, along the Colorado."

"You'd have to stay out of sight. And there's no water back from the river for fifty miles until you get to Deep Well in the Kofas, past Castle Dome Peak. That's why they're having a tough time trying to mine in that area," Heenan said.

"If we all go at once, at least some of us would get out," Ocano reasoned.

In spite of himself, Deraux was beginning to catch escape fever. But they had to have a plan. "If we break for the river and get a log or small boat to float us south, across the border, one or two might make it."

"The law pays fifty dollars a head for every returned prisoner," Gilliland said. "The Yumas and Mojaves are good trackers. They'd have the riverbanks covered, even south of the border. The *rurales* are always on the look-out for smugglers, and the Cocopahs are very good at capturing escaped prisoners. Then there's the steamboat traffic to look out for."

"Going west, across the river, if you slip past the soldiers at Fort Yuma, you've got miles of the desert to contend with," Heenan said. "I know this country roundabout. I was with a group of Mormons who scouted the whole area for possible settlements."

"Strike southeast, then, away from Yuma and the river," Ocano said.

Heenan shook his head. "There's nothing

out there but miles of the hottest damn' desert you can imagine. Probably thirty, forty miles to the first mountains. You might be able to hike across in winter if you had plenty of water and something to eat. But there's no water until you get to Maricopa Wells, more than ninety miles from here. This time of year, you'd be shriveled like a prune before you got a fourth of that distance."

"What about the tanks in the Tinajas Altas Mountains?" Deraux asked.

"Good chance they're dry this time of year."

"I stopped at those tanks once in January," Deraux said. "There was plenty of water, then. But what impressed me was how big some of those hollows in the granite are. It'd take a lot of hot, dry weather to evaporate all the water they held." He recalled the scum-covered, stagnant pools. But at least it was water.

"We've had a long, dry spell," Heenan countered. "You really want to chance it? They say death by thirst is one of the worst tortures that can happen to a man." He gestured at the cramped cell. "This place is no picnic, but at least we have enough to eat, plenty of clean well water to drink, and a cot to sleep on."

"What about along the border?"

Vasquez laughed dryly. "*El Camino del Diablo.* The Devil's Highway. The old *padre*s named it right."

Deraux nodded. The Spaniards had a knack for such descriptive names. 100 miles of burning desert where one had to depend for a drink on *pozitos* dug in sand washes, or *tinajas,* eroded in granite mountains.

"You've already made up your mind to stay and serve your time, *amigo,*" Vasquez said. "I'll never live long enough to see the end of my term. I'm for any plan that has a chance of success."

"If the heat doesn't get you, there are always the Papagos, or maybe wandering Apaches who claim that region, or maybe their Sonoran cousins, the Yaquis," Heenan said encouragingly, playing devil's advocate.

Vasquez spat accurately into the overflowing slop bucket. "*¡Madre de Dios!* Even the Indians avoid that desert this time of year."

"Can you draw us a map of the surrounding area, showing the river and the desert mountains, especially the location of any water?" Deraux asked.

Heenan thought for a moment. "Sure. Get me a pencil and paper."

"I'll steal some paper out of the library," Vasquez said.

Morning light filtered into the stinking cells. Whistles blew. Boots thudded in the passageways. Ratcheting levers loaded Winchester chambers as the guards went to their posts, working in pairs — one to open the cell doors and unchain the inmates from the huge ring set deep into the rock floor, the other to stand watch with ready rifle. A guard at each door opened a heavy padlock with a key. At a signal, the metal bar was thrown that actuated both the inner and outer cell doors. Metallic clanging echoed down the passageways and off the stone walls as all the cells were opened at once. The prisoners were unchained and filed out under the guards' watchful eyes. The men shuffled down the passageway toward the mess hall, yawning, scratching, coughing. Talking was forbidden.

They sat on benches at long tables, eating lumpy mush out of tin bowls with wooden spoons. The prison authorities were careful not to give them anything they could fashion into a weapon. But, at the moment, weapons were not on Deraux's mind. A method of escape was. He softened the Civil War surplus hardtack in the strong black coffee and pondered his next move. Should he go it alone, or combine his escape attempt with the others? He worked better solo. But, here, a single man's efforts would be doomed. On the other hand, could he depend upon the three other men in his cell who were eager to try? Fearless and desperate, Three-Fingered Jack Ocano would be an asset — if he didn't get sidetracked taking revenge on the brutal guard, Big Bill Braxton. Deraux looked across the table at the youthful Gil Gilliland. The Irishman with the black, curly hair was something of a mystery. He was quiet, but had been sentenced for killing a man with his fists over a woman during a drunken brawl. He was careful about his food, drink, exercise and rest — a man who'd been a laborer and an athlete. But Gilliland, chaffing terribly under confinement, was like a spring under tension who'd explode with energy once the break started. For Vasquez, it was all or nothing. He would escape or die in the attempt. Heenan, a prisoner for the non-violent crime of polygamy, making it clear he would remain and serve out his sentence, had promised not to hinder them.

Ignoring what he ate, Deraux spooned up the last of the tasteless mush, and swallowed the last of the bitter coffee as one would stoke a furnace. He considered the meal as nothing more than fuel for his body.

Breakfast finished, the prisoners marched

to their duties for the day. Ocano and Deraux drew their tools and were escorted to the cemetery on a slope overlooking the junction of the Colorado and the Gila Rivers.

"Need four graves," the guard said, pointing with his stubby shotgun. "Start a new row right over here."

"Four? Who died?"

"Don't ask questions. Just dig."

"The chink, for one. Who else?" Ocano persisted boldly.

"Maybe you, if you're out in this sun long enough." The guard sauntered off a few yards and sat down on the big rocks of a mounded grave.

Ocano grunted something under his breath, then swung his pick overhead and brought it down with all the force of his massive body. The point of the pick barely chipped the caliche. Ocano looked at Deraux from under his straw hat. "Shit!" he muttered out of the corner of his mouth.

"Looks like a long job," Deraux whispered back, glancing at the guard who was perched on a grave, cradling his weapon and smoking a cigarette.

The sun cleared the horizon and its oblique rays began stoking up the heat, beginning another day of baking the bare soil rock hard. No rain for months, and none expected until at least October. Less than four inches of rain a year would do nothing to soften the soil in any case. By mutual agreement, the bigger man broke the hard top layer while Deraux shoveled out the detritus. Once they got down a foot or more, Deraux took over wielding the pick.

Deraux looked across the compound at four other prisoners who were chiseling a dark cell into the side of a hill to be used for solitary confinement. From a distance, the prisoners in their uniforms of horizontal black and yellow stripes resembled bumblebees.

It was one of the worst days Deraux could remember. Even though they were given all the water they wanted, mid-afternoon found his head aching and his knees rubbery. He climbed out of the knee-deep hole, wiping his hands on his pants, feeling the blisters between the calluses. He took a deep breath of the heated air and looked across the river to California. Dust devils formed and spun, dissipating into the shimmering heat that rose from the desert floor.

The guards were changed, but he and Ocano were not relieved. Big Bill Braxton sauntered into the graveyard, ironwood club swinging from his belt. Ocano glared his hatred at the stocky guard with the crooked nose.

"Ole Sol ain't got you yet?" Braxton taunted. "He will." He chuckled. "It's just a matter of time."

Ocano opened his mouth to retort, but Deraux stepped quickly between them. "Be quiet," he whispered. "He's trying to goad you into cussing him so he can beat you."

Ocano drew a deep breath and returned to work, transferring his rage to an extra hard pick stroke in the rocky soil.

One of the prisoners at work on the dark cell dropped from sunstroke, and was dragged into the shade to lie until he recovered. At two o'clock another, working on the road leading up from Yuma to the prison, was carried off.

Deraux and Ocano, by rationing their strength, managed to last until supper. But Deraux knew he didn't have many more days like that left in him. The break would have to be soon, or he'd be leaving his bones under the caliche.

For four more days, Deraux worked in the graveyard. Only his hate kept him going when other men fell. Ocano was a machine. When he wasn't cursing, his pick or shovel rose and fell with monotonous regularity. He was either impervious to heat, Deraux decided, or his hate was even stronger and drove him on. Despite eating and drinking as much as they could lay hands on, both men lost weight.

Heenan drew them a map of the surrounding country, marking roads, rivers, desert mountains, and possible water holes. "It's all from memory, but I think it's fairly accurate," Heenan said. He and Deraux then used a tablet filched from the library to make four more copies.

By evening of the fourth day on their grave-digging detail, word of the break had somehow spread to the cells on either side of them and one diagonally across the hall. At least twelve other cons were eager to join.

"The break's gotta come tomorrow," Ocano said after their leg chains were fastened and the doors had clanged shut for the night. "Or else word's gonna leak out to the screws that something's about to happen."

Deraux nodded. "Yeah. One more day with a shovel in that sun could be the end o' me."

"Tomorrow's Saturday and the number of guards will be reduced. Our punishment detail will go on anyway, so we'll be outside," Ocano said.

"We'll try it just before dark," Deraux

said. "There will be a partial moon, but it'll rise late."

The two men fell to discussing details, with Vasquez adding a comment now and then. Gilliland mostly just listened. There was no way successfully to scale the walls. Adobe-plastered stone ten feet thick at the base, tapering to four feet wide at the top, and fifteen feet high, the walls were surmounted with guard towers in the corners. To have a chance, they'd have to get hold of the keys to the doors. When the particulars had been worked out, the plan was whispered to the men in the other cells. It'd take place as the men finished supper and before they were herded back to their cells for the night. When the whistle sounded for the end of the evening meal, the cons would overwhelm the guards, and disarm them. With weapons and keys, the convicts would then open the door leading to the graveyard outside the main compound, and make a break for the brush along the river, shooting anyone who got in their way. If they moved fast enough and with the element of surprise, perhaps some of them would avoid bullets from the Gatling gun and the Winchesters.

The next morning at sunup, Deraux and

Ocano were set to work in the graveyard while the other work gangs were given free time to read or to work on handcrafted items that were sold to the public on Sundays. Although heat and nerves had stolen his appetite, Deraux forced himself to eat as much as he could hold at breakfast and lunch, knowing if he got outside, it might be a long time until the next meal. The two of them were the only laborers working in the graveyard, and only one guard was set over them. That man was Big Bill Braxton who'd given his men Saturday off. He seemed to enjoy watching the two prisoners toil and sweat in the sun while he lounged, smoking a cigarette. He eschewed a shotgun for guard duty, and carried only his holstered Colt. His favorite weapon, the ironwood club, was on his belt.

The sun was sapping Deraux's energy. He pretended to work, but was actually dogging it, saving his strength for later. As the day wore on, the wind picked up, blowing grit off the loaded shovels and into their eyes and mouths. Braxton, who sat downwind of them, finally stood up and moved. The wind grew steadily, rattling gravel against the tool shed and the wooden headboards in the cemetery, raking the adobe walls. Gusts off the surrounding

135

desert swept up layers of powdery particles, whirling them high into the air until the billowing, yellowish dust obscured everything for more than fifty yards. The air smelled of dust, and the men were coated with a fine layer of it, yet it didn't stick to the skin like paste because their perspiration instantly evaporated.

The six o'clock whistle sounded for supper, but Braxton made no move to dismiss the men for the evening meal.

"Ain't we gonna eat, Braxton?" Ocano yelled above the driving wind, leaning on his shovel.

"You got all day tomorrow to lollygag around," the guard said. "Finish that grave before you knock off." Braxton pulled a piece of jerky from his uniform pocket and began gnawing on it.

"Hell, that'll take two more hours!" Ocano said.

"Perfect. It'll be dark, and you'll be done."

"Shit!" Ocano turned his back on the guard and pretended to slam the point of his shovel into the foot-deep hole, but grinned at Deraux as he did so. It was working just as they'd planned. Neither man wanted to go inside.

Another hour dragged by. Braxton took a long drink from the canteen he had slung from his shoulder. The wind continued to fill the air with dust, wrapping Prison Hill in premature twilight. Through the haze, Deraux could barely see the big sheltered guard tower with its Gatling gun.

Somewhere inside, a whistle signaled the end of the supper hour. The two gravediggers paused. Suddenly they heard faint sounds of a struggle and a yell, followed by a shot. The guard leaped to his feet, hand going to his Colt as he turned toward the cell-block. It was a fatal mistake. A second later, the flat of Ocano's shovel struck Big Bill Braxton full in the face with all the power of the big half-breed behind it. The head guard fell without a sound.

Seconds later the iron grate flew open and several prisoners in striped uniforms burst forth, two of them waving pistols. A dozen men scattered among the mounded graves, running like rabbits, bounding down the slope toward the river. After a slight hesitation, the Gatling gun chattered its deadly staccato from the guard tower. Lead slugs ripped across the bare ground, overtaking the fleeing prisoners.

Ocano finished off Braxton by smashing the guard's face with a rock, then dashed away, joining the rush for the river.

Two men flung up their arms and fell, but

Deraux saw no more. He was dragging the body of the guard toward the open grave amidst the cracking of Winchesters and the rhythmic explosions of the Gatling.

In the dust-blown twilight at the bottom of the shallow grave, Deraux stripped off his prison garb and exchanged it for the uniform of the dead guard. They were nearly the same size, and Braxton also had dark hair. The guard's face was unrecognizable, and Deraux hoped it would be an hour or two before they realized the body in the yellow and black stripes was not his.

The long-barreled Colt .45 was fully loaded and the loops of the cartridge belt held another twenty-four rounds. He peered cautiously above the hole. Dusk was coming on, and blowing dust obscured details. Gunfire from the towers had ceased and he saw several striped mounds — bodies of cons cut down. These few had not reached the cover of the brush along the riverbank, but had, nonetheless, escaped.

He waited as long as he dared, hoping for darkness. But a manual search would soon begin. Three minutes later the gunfire was becoming sporadic and distant. He bellied out of the grave and lay still for several seconds, watching and listening. Finally he rose, tugged the kepi down on his head, and trotted toward the lower end of the sloping graveyard, pistol in hand, hoping to be mistaken for a guard if he were seen from one of the watchtowers. There was a shout from behind, but he didn't stop, plunging into the brush and sliding on down the hill toward the riverbank.

Suddenly he realized men were in the river and guards were yelling directions at each other, running along the bank, shooting at heads bobbing in the water.

Taking advantage of the noise and confusion, Deraux changed course and started through the mesquite away from the river and toward Yuma. The uproar of the break out would have guards swarming the streets of the town as well as the banks of the river. If he were caught in Braxton's uniform, he'd be arrested for murder.

At the corner of the first street, he paused to holster his Colt, catch his breath, and brush the dust off his uniform. Ocano had bolted away on his own, waiting for him as one hog at a trough waits for another. That was all right with Deraux. It was every man for himself now.

Where to go? He knew no one here. If any of the off-duty guards were in town and had heard the noise of the break, they'd be on the look-out. Any of the guards would quickly recognize him as a phony.

From somewhere down the block came the faint music of a concertina. He darted across the street into an alleyway. A rat scurried away from his footfalls. Rotting garbage overflowed trash barrels, its ripe stench mingling with the smell of privies behind a row of saloons.

The streets began to fill with people, and Deraux stepped into the shadows of a doorway as two men came down the alley, talking in Spanish and sharing a bottle. He was thankful for the darkness and the blowing dust. He had to find some other clothing before the Saturday night revelers became too numerous in this part of town.

A pair of uniformed guards turned into the alley, one carrying a lantern. They worked their way toward him, swinging their clubs, peering into privies, and behind barrels and empty boxes.

Deraux felt a moment of panic as he pressed back into the doorway. He had to hide. Perhaps he could rip off the cap and jacket, and lie down like a drunk who's passed out. But then they'd recognize him as an escaped prisoner by his close-cropped hair, or his face, if they were guards he knew.

He had to make a quick decision. They were within ten yards of him. He dropped his hand to the Colt. But the sound of shots in this alley would bring the law running. He could surprise and overpower one guard, but not two, before the alarm was given.

He held his breath and prepared to spring.

CHAPTER EIGHT

As Deraux crouched, his shoulder bumped the door behind him. To his surprise, the door gave and swung silently inward on oiled hinges. He glanced at the approaching guards. The light of their bull's-eye lantern probed here and there behind the litter as it swung toward him, hardly a dozen feet away. He had no choice. Colt in hand, he quickly ducked inside the dark room and pushed the door nearly shut behind him.

"We could be waylaid in this damned alley," one of the guards growled, their light flashing across the now empty doorway.

"Yeah. Keep your eyes open and your gun handy," the other man replied as their footsteps and voices began to recede.

Deraux took a deep breath, trying to calm his pounding heart. He leaned weakly against the wall. Where was he? The room was completely dark, but, as his eyes adjusted, he could make out a dim light showing through a muslin-draped doorway leading to the next room. He holstered his pistol and, hands extended, cautiously groped his way toward the light. He bumped into a low bed and a chair, but made almost no noise, finally pausing at the curtained doorway. The odor of stale cigar smoke and perfume hung in the stuffy room. A Mexican woman sat in an armchair, filing her fingernails by the light of a coal-oil lamp. She was in a dressing gown and her wavy hair fell to her shoulders, reflecting a black sheen in the lamplight. From what he could see of her face, he got a quick impression of sultry good looks, made puffy by dissipation.

Something moved on the other side of the room and Deraux leaned back into the shadow. A lean man was asleep on the sagging couch across the room from the woman. He stirred and mumbled something in his sleep.

Deraux guessed he was in the crib of a prostitute, possibly in the rear of some saloon. He slid away toward the door he'd entered. Time to go. The guards should be gone by now. It was doubtful they'd search the alley a second time. Then he hesitated. Could he get out of Yuma wearing the guard's uniform? Better than prison stripes, but the garb would surely call attention to him.

He carefully felt his way to the door, opened it a foot, and slipped out, closing it softly behind him. The moon was rising and the wind had died, although the air still smelled of dust.

Deraux tried to get his bearings. He had to avoid the river where most of the other prisoners had fled and the searchers were concentrated. And he would need water if he was going to strike southeast into the desert. He paused and tugged the cap down on his head. The moon gave pale illumination to the littered alleyway.

He was startled by thudding footsteps and turned to see a bulky figure lumbering toward him. Deraux brought up his Colt, the barrel glinting in the moonlight. The man slowed, snatched something off a nearby trash heap, and swung it at him. Deraux ducked, firing blindly. The board glanced off his shoulder, striking him in the ear. His cap went flying and he fell on his back, head reeling. Before he could cock the revolver, the bulky form leaped and pinned him. He heard harsh breathing and smelled sweat.

Suddenly the door behind them opened and lamplight flooded the struggling pair.

"*¿Quién es?*" quavered a woman's voice.

Yellow light fell full on the flushed musta-chioed face a foot from Deraux's eyes.

"Ocano!" Deraux gasped through the chokehold. "It's me . . . Deraux."

The attacker's eyes went wide. "Son-of-a-bitch!" He released his grip and drew back. "Thought you was one o' them damned screws."

The woman who'd opened the door moved to close it, but the big man rolled upright and thrust a big boot in the way. "Hold it, lady, we're coming in." Ocano dragged Deraux to his feet as if he weighed nothing. The board had left a slight cut on his ear and a rising swelling on the side of his head.

Deraux rubbed his bruised throat as he stumbled back inside. The phenomenal grip of his former cellmate had nearly crushed his windpipe. He recognized the woman he'd been spying on a few minutes earlier. She led the way through the bedchamber and through the muslin curtain into the sitting area. The drunk was stirring on the couch.

"Lady, get this man some clothes," Ocano said, indicating Deraux.

"I have none, *señor*," she said. Her hand shook as she placed the lamp on the table.

She turned to the lean Mexican now sitting and rubbing the sleep from his red eyes while looking bewildered. "Rivera, where can this man get a pair of pants and a shirt?" she asked.

"I do not know," he said.

Deraux, who was standing closest, could smell the whiskey on his breath. A nearly empty bottle lay on the floor by the couch.

"Shit!" Ocano spat, looking at the Mexican's lean frame. "He could swap with you, but you're too damned skinny." He glanced around the tiny room, then settled on Deraux. "You and me gotta get the hell outta here. That shot'll bring the law." He gnawed indecisively at the corner of his mustache. His baldhead glistened with sweat in the lamplight. He grabbed the woman's arm. "What's your name, *chiquita?*"

"Elena."

"Get us two or three canteens of water . . . *pronto!*"

She jumped.

"Hold it." Ocano swept up the bottle from the floor and emptied it with a swallow. "Here, fill this with water, too. I'll be watching you, so don't say a word about us being here, or I'll kill you. *¿Comprende?*"

"*Sí, señor.*" Her eyes were wide. "I swear

146

on the Virgin of Guadalupe."

"You'd better swear on your own life, 'cause that's what you'll lose if you give us away."

"You have my word."

She opened the door to the saloon, letting in the clamor of voices, laughter, and clinking glassware. Ocano flattened himself against the wall and caught the door, holding it open a crack so he could watch the girl.

Deraux kept his gaze on Rivera. He suspected the Mexican was not nearly as befuddled with drink as he let on. From the looks of these quarters, Deraux assumed Elena had just finished with this client.

Elena returned in five minutes with three canteens and the whiskey bottle full of water. She handed the bottle and the heavy containers to Ocano. "I told the bartender I needed the water to wash myself," she said.

"Who're you?" Ocano asked the Mexican.

"Angel Rivera."

"What's the shortest way out of town?"

Rivera pointed toward the alley.

"How far?"

"Half a mile to the edge of the desert." Rivera looked as if he wanted to throw up from fear or a sour stomach. "You are the *hombres* from the prison, no?"

"How far to water?" Ocano demanded, ignoring the question.

"A day, *mas o menos.*"

"Speak English! How far in miles?"

"About thirty or forty miles, more or less, to the high tanks in the first mountains."

"You know the way?"

Rivera nodded, swallowing, his prominent Adam's apple bobbing up and down.

"You'll guide us there."

"But *señor,* I am not a well man. The heat . . . the tanks might be dry this time of year."

"And you might be lying, you little weasel!" Ocano jerked him to his feet by his shirtfront, and backhanded him across the mouth. Rivera's head snapped sideways and his fearful expression changed to one of rage.

"Look out!" Deraux yelled.

A knife flashed from the Mexican's boot top and the blade whipped up just as the big half-breed jerked back. Ocano's shirtfront was ripped open and a fine trickle of blood oozed from a foot-long cut on his hairy chest.

"Ah, you strike quicker than a sidewinder, *amigo.*" He grinned, showing big white teeth below the bushy mustache. "But you'll have reason to regret that."

Rivera crouched in a defensive posture, holding the blade up for another slash or thrust.

Deraux cocked the Colt, the double *click* of the hammer loud in the sudden silence.

"No, no, don't shoot the little bastard," Ocano said. "He's defiant as a cornered rat. But we need him as a live rat, not a dead one." He held out his hand. "I'll take that before it gets you into any more trouble."

Rivera, eyeing the long-barreled Colt trained on him, handed over the knife, haft forward. Ocano shoved the weapon under his belt.

Elena, who'd backed into a corner, reached into a woven bag on the floor and brought out a full whiskey bottle. "Here, *señor,* please take this and go, before someone comes."

"Ah, my little *puta,* you read my mind." The big man pulled the cork with his teeth, then took three huge swallows. *"Whoogh!"* He drizzled the ninety-proof liquid down the cut on his chest, catching his breath as he did so. "And now, we'll bid you a good evening, with thanks for your hospitality," Ocano said, recorking the bottle and handing it back to Elena. He turned toward the Mexican. "You! Rivera! Out the door. You will pay for your indiscretion by acting as

149

our guide across the desert to the nearest water . . . and beyond."

"*Por favor, señor* . . . I meant nothing by it. I reacted only. It was . . . a mistake."

"You're damned right it was a mistake, and you're about to pay for it."

"Please don't make me go with you into that . . . place. Even the Apaches do not go there in August. It is the very flames of hell itself. No man can live. . . ."

"Let's go!" Ocano jerked the whiner to his feet and flung him toward the door. "Get moving! We can be twenty miles from here by daylight." He handed one of the full canteens to Deraux, who had holstered his weapon. Ocano yanked open the door, thrust his head out, and looked up and down. "All clear." He shoved Rivera out into the moonlight. "If he tries to run, shoot him," he said to Deraux." He turned back. "*Adiós,* Elena. If I only had a little time, what you and I could do. . . ." He sighed and shoved Rivera ahead of him.

Deraux stripped off the uniform jacket, wadded it up and flung it over a fence behind a privy. With no hat, only dark blue pants and his long underwear top, he would not be mistaken for a guard. His cropped hair identified him as a prisoner, but they would have to steal some hats, anyway,

150

before challenging the desert. "Shadrack, Meshack, and Abednego," he muttered to himself.

"What'd you say?" Ocano asked.

"Nothing."

With Rivera between them, they turned out of the alley and started east along the dusty street. Deraux realized their long, slim chance at escape had only begun.

They zigzagged through back streets and alleyways, keeping to the shadows and away from pedestrians and the light of saloons and stores. In a pool of light spilling from the kitchen door of a restaurant, they surprised four Mexicans shooting craps. The sudden appearance of Deraux's blue-black Colt persuaded three of them to part with their straw hats. As an afterthought, Ocano scooped up the pot of greenbacks and silver *pesos* from the ground.

"*Adiós, muchachos,*" the big half-breed growled, grinning as the trio faded into the night. From there, they moved quickly toward the eastern edge of town.

"Taking that money wasn't smart," Deraux said. "They'll sound the alarm and the guards will be after us."

"Maybe. Maybe not." Ocano seemed unconcerned. "Even if they do, they won't know where we went. Besides, the guards will never follow us into the desert."

"Hell, no," Deraux panted as they jogged along in the dark. "The Yuma trackers will be glad to do it for fifty dollars a head."

"Scared?"

Deraux could almost see the big man grinning in the dark. "Not so's you could notice it." Deraux shoved the lagging Rivera ahead of him. "We got our Mex, here, to guide us to water."

"Hope he knows where he's going," Ocano said.

"If he doesn't, we'll all die together."

They slowed to a fast walk, catching their breath as they passed the last scattered adobes where Yuma trickled into the desert. Deraux had the impression of a limitless ocean rolling away to the east; a sudden qualm gripped his stomach. Yet he knew this was, for now, the safest direction away from pursuit. The other prisoners had run for the Colorado, and the search would be concentrated up and down the river. The guards knew it was suicide for anyone to attempt to cross the desert on foot. One or two of the escapees might walk the railroad bridge into California, but a lot of desert awaited them there as well.

"How many of the other boys got away?" Deraux asked.

152

"Vasquez won't have to worry about drowning in the river. He was cut down in the graveyard along with a chink and another man I didn't stop to notice," Ocano said. "Last I saw of Gilliland, he was swimming like hell for the California shore." Ocano paused and uncorked a canteen, taking two or three deep swallows.

"Better go easy on that water," Deraux said. "We got a long way to go."

"I ain't got to this point in my life by being told what to do."

Deraux shrugged. They had three two-quart canteens and one quart whiskey bottle full of water to see the three of them through to the next water, many miles away. He had one of the canteens slung from his own shoulder and would make sure it stayed there, if he had to defend it with his Colt from the big man. Ocano was bull-headed and would take what he wanted, regardless. During the several months Deraux had known the half-breed, the big man had not shown loyalty to anyone but himself.

Ocano corked the canteen, and the trio trudged silently away through the sandy hillocks.

Deraux glanced at the glittering ice chips of stars. The moon would shed some light for a few hours yet. They had to make time

153

before daylight. There would be no resting for them. He wondered if the indefatigable Ocano was as sore and tired as he.

Their boots shuffled forward through the sand, each step taking them farther from the brutal guards and the choking, deadening confinement of Yuma prison. Yet it was also taking them farther from life-giving water and food, and into the temporarily dead furnace of the nighttime desert.

Hour after hour they trudged, single file, Rivera leading, Ocano second, and Deraux bringing up the rear. Except for the scuffing of their boots and their husky breathing, it was totally silent — a lifeless place.

Deraux turned and looked back. He was dismayed at how close the lights of Yuma still appeared to be. He thought of the rushing, fresh water of the Colorado, pouring thousands of gallons an hour downstream to empty into the salty Gulf of California. The tiny portion of water they carried was slung over their shoulders like life vests for ocean travelers.

The ground became less sandy and more crowded with desert scrub as it gradually sloped upward.

Ocano had assumed command by sheer force of will and dominant strength. As long as Deraux had the Colt, he chose not to

154

waste energy by disputing authority with the big half-breed who, as far as Deraux knew, was armed only with Rivera's knife. Ocano stopped and they all paused to sip water from the canteens. Deraux was careful not to let Rivera have more than a swallow.

"Gimme some more," Rivera gasped as Deraux yanked the canteen away, sloshing a little on the ground.

"Shut up, you whining bastard!" Ocano said.

That was the extent of the conversation as they started again, quickly falling into a rhythmic, trance-like pace.

The moon set, and, except for the faraway stars, there was no light at all. No one lived in that country, and almost no one crossed this way, normally taking the Gila Trail, miles to the north. Besides the water of the Gila, that route also provided danger of capture, of torture and of death at the hands of the dreaded Apaches, or bandits, both American and Mexican.

A slight movement of air crept across the desert, a forerunner of the dawn. The husking of their boots on the harsh earth, and their labored breathing continued without pause. Ahead of them, the mountains in the distance were discernible only by where their humped backs blotted out the stars.

Deraux's legs were like stone; he struggled to lift them, first one, then the other. The all day hard labor with pick and shovel, the tension and strain of the break out, the eluding of capture in Yuma, and the all night trek in the desert had sapped his strength. He'd had no food or rest for at least thirty-six hours, and now dawn was approaching. Dawn — normally a glad, refreshing time of day. But he knew, and feared, what was to follow.

The sky grew slowly lighter, and the mountains were closer. Or were they? He began to feel as if he were on a treadmill, the dry land running back beneath the thin soles of his boots, the mountains as far away as ever.

Suddenly it was light and he could see the great folds of the mountains. Each scant desert bush stood out clearly, as evenly spaced as if they'd been planted by man instead of Nature. The eastern sky flowed from dark gray to lighter gray, to pearly gray; the tops of the rounded mountains stood out starkly in the dry, clear air.

"Hold it," Ocano said, breathing heavily. "Take a break." He pulled the whiskey water bottle from his pocket, popped the cork, and gulped down most of the water it contained. He looked at Rivera in the early light. "By God, I didn't see those before." He reached out and snatched three slim cigars from the shirt pocket of the Mexican. He bit off the end of one, and said: "Gimme a match."

Rivera complied and the big man lit up.

The aroma of cigar smoke in the fresh air seemed to reconnect the wild desert to man, Deraux thought. Not surprisingly Ocano didn't offer to share the cigars.

"If those are the mountains we're headed for, we got a little off track in the dark." Ocano pointed toward the gray-green folds of a mountain to the northeast.

"No, *señor*," Rivera replied. "Those are the Gilas. There is no water there. We must reach the Tinajas Altas Mountains. There." He pointed.

"Shit!" The big half-breed couldn't hide his shock as he gazed at the distant mountains, low in the southeast. His ruddy face had taken on a gray cast in the dawn light.

"The tanks are on the east side," Rivera continued.

"How far?"

"Thirty miles."

Ocano seemed to get a grip on himself. His eyes narrowed and he puffed on the cigar, blowing clouds of white smoke that drifted off on the light morning breeze. It was still relatively cool, even as the blazing orb shoved its head above the eastern horizon with a silent explosion of light. The new day had begun.

"We'd better get moving," Deraux said after several seconds of silence.

"I'll say when we go," Ocano retorted. He sat down heavily on the ground, and proceeded to finish his smoke.

Deraux glanced at Rivera. The Mexican had a wolfish look on his lean face, as if he'd just seen his bigger, stronger prey begin to weaken. Deraux took off his straw hat and raked his fingers through his hair. Then he hunkered down, stretching his back muscles, giving his tired legs a rest. He didn't want to sit down for fear he wouldn't want to get up again. And he was averse to showing any weakness in front of Rivera, who was still standing.

The aromatic cigar smoke smelled better than Deraux's own dusty, sweat-soaked clothing. He was so weary, he could have stretched out and gone to sleep on the spot. But that would have meant certain death; there was no shade for miles — only some tiny desert shrubs. He knew the worst part of their trek was just beginning. They had less than six quarts of water among them.

He uncorked his canteen and tipped it up, swishing the water around in his mouth before swallowing. Not enough to replenish the moisture he was losing, but just enough to fool his mouth and throat.

"Water, *señor?*" Rivera asked, holding out a hand.

Deraux passed the canteen to him, watching carefully as the Mexican drank. "Enough!" He sprang up and grabbed the canteen as Rivera took a second large swallow.

"I must have water," the Mexican said.

"You're the smallest one here," Deraux said. "You need less than any of us."

"If I die, you will not find the tanks," Rivera said softly.

"That damned whiskey has dried you out," Deraux said. "I'll give you enough water to keep you going. We're all going to make it."

Ocano flipped away his cigar butt, then rolled to his hands and knees and pushed himself slowly to his feet like a bull buffalo.

With no more conversation, they started again, facing the rising sun. The slanting rays struck Deraux's face, feeling for the skin, probing for the moisture within. Like the hull of a ship that holds out the deadly sea, his envelope of skin and thin clothing would have to hold out the deadly rays of the sun. It would start with his exposed face and hands, searing the flesh, cracking the lips, burning the eyes, striking through the cloth of the white underwear shirt and the dark pants.

They plodded southeast, heads down, hat brims shading eyes, puffs of dust rising with every step. A half hour later the ground began to heat up. Deraux felt it through his thin soles and worn socks. The sweat and dust worked together, stinging his eyes, coating his cracked lips, working up into his nostrils, causing a gritty, salty taste in his mouth. Now and then, he glanced over his shoulder. All sign of Yuma had passed over the horizon. He half expected to see pursuing Yuma trackers. But there was no one. If the guards knew what direction they'd taken, perhaps they assumed the desert would do their work for them. The three of them were committed. They had reached the point of no return. It was either go forward and find water, or die in the attempt.

They passed the last of the scant growth of shrubs and faced an expanse of crusted earth, whitened by salt deposits — perhaps the bed of a lake dried up before man had appeared on the great desert. It was cracked and interlaced by furrows where rains had beaten on the thin crust in times past, maybe even covering the harsh earth with a sheet of water for a time. The sun would have its way, as it always did, drying up the water, then the mud, then driving what little moisture was left deep down into the ground, cracking the dried upper crust.

Deraux found a big, dirty bandanna in the pocket of the uniform pants and tied it around his nose and mouth in a feeble attempt to protect his skin from the rays reflecting up from the whitened lake bed, and to filter some of the heat and dust from his lungs. The cloth over his face was nearly stifling, but better than what was out there, he thought, slitting his eyes at the wavering heat waves rising from the sunbaked earth. How much farther, he wondered. Rivera had said thirty miles. How fast were they walking? Perhaps three miles an hour. Ten hours to the tanks. Three hours since sunrise. They'd covered less than a third of the distance, and Ocano had drained the rest of the water in the whiskey bottle and one of the two-quart canteens he carried. He left it to Deraux to share his one canteen with Rivera. More moisture was being sucked from their bodies by the furnace heat than was being replaced. Even if they survived sunstroke, Deraux estimated they'd need at least three gallons of water apiece to make this crossing. Fourteen or fifteen hours of daylight this time of year. Before dark they would be at the safety of the tanks, or they'd be running wildly, out of their minds, only to fall, belly down, their bleeding hands clawing senselessly at the sandy earth for water that was not there.

While Deraux's vision of the ever-retreating Tinajas Altas Mountains was blurred by wavering heat waves, he turned his sight inward and with his mind's eye saw the flowing water tap in the mess hall at Yuma prison. There was always plenty of fresh water there. Mormon Bob Heenan was still there, drinking his fill, then going to lie down on his bunk in the shady cell. Heenan had been wise not to join the break. But, then, he had only a few more months to serve.

The sun crept overhead and began its long, torturous slide toward the western horizon behind them. But, to Deraux, the fiery brass ball was fastened to the sky, so slowly did it seem to move. The heat radiated like a blast furnace, too intense and painful to be ignored by thinking of other things. His head throbbed, and he stumbled forward, automatically placing one foot ahead of the other, disconnected from the thought of walking. He sensed he was on the verge of sunstroke, and longed to pour the rest of the canteen over his head to cool himself. But he was still rational enough to know if he were to survive, he must only sip the water. He was not even aware of the other two men as he paused and uncorked the canteen, poured a little past his parched lips, swishing the warm, metallic-tasting water around in his mouth before spitting it back into the canteen. He shook the canvas-covered container, estimating it contained less than a pint. It was some relief to lubricate his mouth, but his body cried out for more moisture, for floods of cooling water. He swigged another mouthful, swirled it around, and swallowed.

Rivera and Ocano trudged ahead, unaware he'd stopped. Deraux started forward, but made no attempt to catch up.

The fear of capture no longer bothered him. It was a remote danger, compared to the fierce natural enemy that had them locked in mortal combat. But Deraux relied on his will to live and his cunning to see him through.

He had not figured on his weakness.

CHAPTER NINE

Deraux slid in and out of consciousness, automatically shuffling one foot ahead of the other, boots husking on the parched earth. His mind wandered, disconnected from present time and place.

He caught his toe on a half-buried rock and tumbled forward like a disjointed puppet, tearing the knees out of his pants, and bruising the heels of his hands as he broke his fall on the scorching earth. Jolted back to the present, he started to rise, but discovered that it required great effort, as if his arms and legs were not used to working together. Erect again and swaying, he sensed the blisters burned on the bottoms of his feet through the worn boot soles and socks.

Pulling down the bandanna, he sucked in deep breaths of the lung-withering air. Several rods ahead, two dark figures continued bobbing away from him, their outlines blurry through the shimmering heat waves.

Deraux looked over his shoulder — nothing on their back trail but a wavering dust devil silently skipping and spinning across the uneven desert.

In a flash of clarity, he knew he was going to die here. Years from now, some lone traveler on this anvil of the sun would stumble across his bleached bones scattered by scavenging buzzards.

He had no choice but to keep going. He shuffled forward again, breathing heavily, eyes squinted against the blinding glare.

Suddenly a great weakness engulfed him and he felt himself falling into a black hole.

Consciousness returned slowly. He opened his eyes, but could see nothing. Was he dead? No. The hard ground pressing against his cheek told him he was still in the physical world. Darkness had fallen.

With a great effort, he pushed up to a sitting position, pausing for a wave of dizziness to pass. Moonlight was silvering the landscape. He brushed sand from the parched skin of his face. His cracked lips were crusty, and he reached for his canteen. It was gone. He searched the ground around him, but the bright moonlight revealed only scuffmarks and footprints in the sand. The boot prints were too big to be Rivera's.

Ocano. The big man had seen him fall and come back to rob him of his last half pint of water. His gun belt was also missing.

"The bastard should have put a bullet in my head and been done with it," he muttered aloud. In the enveloping stillness his voice rasped like dry cornhusks. He fumbled on the ground and found a smooth pebble to place in his mouth. He'd heard this sometimes started some saliva. It didn't. He was too dry.

His feet felt as if they were glued to the insides of his boots. Fearing his feet were a mass of broken blisters and blood, he tugged at his left boot. But he lacked the strength to remove it.

Hate began to seethe up from deep within him. He would live to get that damned Ocano, somehow.

Struggling unsteadily to his feet, he spat out the dry pebble. No one in sight. From the looks of things, he might have been the last human on a deserted planet. The Tinajas Altas Mountains loomed up ahead, how close he couldn't tell. The dry air and the moonlight made distances deceiving. He put on his straw hat, took a deep breath, and began walking. Hate fueled his strength. He was determined not only to reach the tanks, but to catch up with the pair who'd robbed and abandoned him for dead and kill them both. Plotting and imagining just how he would do this furnished his mind with something to work on as he trudged forward, tongue swollen, throat burning, unable to swallow. His sensitive skin prickled under his clothing, as if he were covered with fine sand. Probably grains of salt from dried perspiration. The sunburned skin of his face felt stretched across his cheek bones and forehead.

I'm dried out, he thought. *If I don't find water soon, I'm a dead man.*

By the time the moon was on the wane, he'd stumbled onto a faintly rutted road that trended along the eastern side of the mountains. But to his left, winding through the scattered greasewood and ocotillo, was another faint trail. He paused to examine it. This trail was not marked by wheels, but by the hoofs of animals — and the boots of men.

He walked up the steadily rising slope, the moon lighting the barely discernible trail. Higher and higher. There was no wind, no movement. His harsh breathing sounded loud in the silence. The sandy soil gave way to rocks that were still warm from heat absorbed during the day. Now boulders humped up from the flank of the mountain.

He looked back across the silvery desert. This was his last chance. He wouldn't survive another day without water. Where were Ocano and Rivera? Lying dead, or unconscious out there? They'd robbed and left him to the mercy of the sun. Now the desert may have claimed them as well.

His weakness was apparent as he paused to catch his breath and rest his legs, aching from the climb. Where was the water? He'd been this way once before, a long time ago, but everything looked different now, especially in the dark. He might have to wait until daylight to scout for the tanks.

Something moved. Something *splashed!* He ran awkwardly toward the sound. Some creature flashed past him, running for shelter in the rocks and brush. Mesquite branches raked his face, knocking off his hat. He paused, panting, and stared intently left and right, his vision trying to penetrate the deep shadows. Then he looked down the slope. Right below him was a great hole in the smooth granite. It was rounded and several yards across. The last of the moonlight reflected off the pewter-colored surface of the water that appeared to be covered with algae and dust. He stumbled forward, dropped to his knees to sweep the surface clean. Then he scooped up a double handful of water and drank, then drank some more. *Thank God!* He didn't slow down to taste the water as it flowed into his mouth and down his throat. His tissues soaked up the moisture like parched desert soil. He splashed it into his face, then plunged his whole head under, rinsing the dust and sand out of his nose and eyes and hair. Finally he sagged down weakly on the warm rocks.

The moonlight was gone when he rolled over, put his mouth to the surface, and sucked up more of the life-giving liquid. This time he tasted the gamey flavor, but he ignored it. This was life or death — no time to be squeamish. But he was glad he couldn't see the wigglers, the tiny pink bladders, the water spiders — all the tiny creatures he knew inhabited this pool.

He finally stopped drinking, feeling his stomach beginning to rebel. He'd drunk too much, too fast. To keep from throwing up, he carefully crept away upslope and lay, face down, on the smooth rock under some bushes to rest his stomach. His stomach relaxed.

In his exhausted state he dozed. When he awoke, the sky was just beginning to gray with coming day. He got up, feeling stiff and sore, and started downhill toward the big tank for another drink. The water had started his gastric juices flowing and a healthy hunger gnawed at his stomach.

He froze, staring down toward the largest tank. A warm, pre-dawn breeze ruffled the leaves of the shrubs. An animal wariness he never knew he possessed alerted him to danger. Was it just the movement of some nocturnal animal — a mule deer, perhaps, or a peccary? He sniffed the slight breeze and caught only the faint, dry scent of sage.

Then a chill went up his back as he found himself staring at the silhouettes of two hatless men standing on the edge of the largest tank. He didn't move, he didn't twitch, but felt his eyes widening to take in every particle of light the coming dawn provided. His ears picked up the guttural sound of voices. He couldn't make out the words, but it didn't sound like English. And white men did not go hatless in this country.

Deraux shrank back and silently melted into the brush, crouching, carefully placing each foot, holding his breath, hoping the slight upslope breeze would carry the sour odor of his sweat-soaked clothing away from the two men. His heart thudded in his ears, shutting out other small sounds. Who were these men? Possibly only wandering Papagos. Everyone who crossed this desert knew of, and used, these high tanks. But the pair

170

might also be Yuma trackers. He felt certain the alarm had gone out far and wide about the prison break. If *any* of the prisoners made good their escape, it would damage the reputation of the Yuma pen as a man-breaker from which no one left alive without serving his sentence.

Then a horse whinnied as if sensing the nearby water. If these were Indian trackers, they'd likely crossed the desert by night on horseback, using moonlight to trail the three fleeing prisoners.

Regardless of where the trail of Ocano and Rivera led, the Indians would have to break off pursuit to stop here for water. Their horses would need a lot of water, and the men would have to replenish their own. Where were the other two prisoners? Could it be these Indians were following his own solitary trail? He shuddered at the thought. With a standard reward of $50 for each returned prisoner, it was very likely these trackers would not return without all three of the escapees in custody, dead or alive.

The two Indians he'd spotted had apparently come ahead on foot to scout the tanks for danger before bringing up the horses. How many of them were in the party, he couldn't tell, but guessed four or five. If he were discovered and still had his Colt and cartridge belt, he'd stand a least a fighting chance.

Before the light grew any stronger, he glided back into the shelter of the boulders, picking his way carefully to avoid making the slightest sound. Lying down in the cover of the jumbled rocks, he barely kept sight of the largest tank between two creosote bushes. By turning his head, he could see the rosy sky as the rising sun lit up the tops of the Cabezas Prietas to the east. On the desert below could be seen the Camino del Diablo snaking its way among the scattered mesquite and occasional organ pipe cactus. Above and behind him loomed the heights of the Tinajas Altas. A low bird whistle sounded from the tanks and was repeated somewhere downslope. Deraux watched as three more Indians led the tired animals up to drink. With any luck, they were only passing through and were not trackers. But he knew it was probably wishful thinking. The tracks he and Ocano and Rivera had made would have been easy to follow. If these Indians had lost the trail in the hard rocks, all they had to do was to sit at the tanks and look out across the heat-soaked desert toward the hazy Cabezas Prietas, and nothing could move out there during the day without being seen by those keen eyes. Or they could wait for him and the other two escapees to stagger up to the tanks, half dead of thirst and too weak to resist.

As the sun rose higher and struck the eastern flank of the Tinajas Altas, Deraux wormed his way deeper into the shade. Then it became a waiting game. Hour after hour passed, and he knew the Indians would not move until dark. Curled up like snakes in the hot shade, they'd await the relative coolness of night before moving out. In the meantime, Deraux began to feel like a loaf of bread in a bake oven as the sun heated up the surrounding rocks. The water he'd drunk came out through his pores and instantly evaporated. He couldn't remember the last time he'd urinated. A powerful thirst returned to torture him. His mouth and throat burned, but he wasn't yet in the extreme condition of the night before. In spite of his resolve to stay alert, his weary, tormented body slipped into a heat-induced doze.

When he awoke, the sun had probed his shaded nook, and his open mouth was dry. He licked his cracked lips and crawled back into the shade, noting the sun had slid toward the western horizon, and shadows were growing long. He heard voices. Then the blast of a gunshot made him jump. But there were no more shots or shouts or signs of a struggle. He rested his throbbing head on his forearms and waited. The sun finally disappeared, streaking the blue sky with red and gold. The smell of wood smoke drifted up to him, followed shortly by the aroma of roasting meat. Apparently they'd slaughtered a horse or the mule. His stomach growled loudly. He was weak from hunger and thirst, but could do nothing until they left.

Under cover of deepening dusk, he bellied forward until he could see the five Indians sitting around their campfire, gorging themselves on half-cooked chunks of bloody meat. He was nearly faint from hunger.

From their shorter hair, along with odds and ends of white man's clothing and knee-high desert moccasins, these men resembled the Yumas that Deraux had seen around the prison. One of the Indians stood up, wiping his hands on his sleeveless shirt, and moved toward the tethered horses. He kicked at something and it was then Deraux saw a man lying trussed on the ground. The man didn't react. Deraux focused intently. Even in the gathering gloom, there was no mistaking the naked barrel chest, bullet head, and huge mustache. It was Ocano. The big man was a prisoner, perhaps injured or wounded.

Unless the trackers had surprised him, the big man would have put up a fight to avoid capture. Did they also have Rivera? Deraux saw no sign of him. The wily Mexican was either dead or had somehow eluded the trackers. It was likely they'd keep Ocano alive for the trip back so they wouldn't have to haul a stinking carcass in the heat. Deraux had no feelings for Ocano, but realized the big half-breed was in for some rough treatment at the hands of his captors. Following Ocano's return, he'd be punished by solitary confinement in the so-called dark cell, where he could easily go mad with no company, no bunk, nothing to do or read, and barely enough to eat. The big half-breed might even face a noose for killing the head guard, if anyone had witnessed the murder in the confusion of the break. Deraux wondered if the Indians had also confiscated the Colt and gun belt, along with the canteens Ocano carried. He lay still, pondering his next move.

He didn't have long to wait. The Indians, talking and laughing, finished eating and tossed the remnants of the meat into the glowing coals of the fire. The meat sizzled as the grease flared up. By the flickering flames Deraux saw the bronzed faces and bodies moving, untying the horses. They swung the full canteens over their shoulders on long straps. He waited impatiently as they hoisted Ocano across the back of a horse and tied his wrists and ankles together beneath the animal's belly. An argument broke out with harsh, guttural voices and much gesturing — an obvious disagreement as to who had to ride behind the prisoner to steady his weight on the horse. Finally one of them vaulted up behind Ocano, and then they guided their mounts downhill and out of Deraux's sight.

Deraux breathed a sigh of relief as the last sounds of their passing died away. He was certain all five had departed, but, to be sure one of their number hadn't slipped back to lay a trap at the campsite, he forced himself to wait and listen and watch another quarter hour before he moved.

Finally assured, he cautiously, noiselessly crept down toward the fire. With a stick, he raked out a half-raw, half-charred hunk of meat, blew on it, then tore at it ravenously with his teeth. The juice ran down his stubbled chin and arms. He rescued another piece and ate it. Then he stirred up the fire so he could see by a small flame, found a bone and cracked it open with a rock to suck out the marrow. He'd never tasted anything as delicious as fresh roasted mule, he thought as he leaned back against a boulder and breathed a long sigh, wiping his hands on his filthy blue uniform trousers. His shrunken stomach was full. Life was good, after all. He got up and walked several yards to the edge of the big tank, and lay down on his belly for a long drink of water.

He heard a slight scuffing noise behind him. A chill went up his back and he whipped around to face this unseen threat. He heard the double *click* of a cocking pistol, and froze.

"Ah, *señor,* I see you've already eaten without me," a familiar voice said. "I was hoping we might have supper together, since this is your last meal." An oily laugh followed and a figure holding a revolver stepped into the faint firelight. It was Rivera.

CHAPTER TEN

Hugh Deraux felt nauseated. All his caution had been for naught. He was so concerned about the Indians, he'd failed to watch for the missing Mexican, assuming he was either dead, holed up, or running like a rabbit.

"Well, if it isn't Angel Rivera," he said, trying to appear nonchalant — and failing. He stood up. "How'd you escape those redskins?" He eyed the Colt with studied disinterest as if he hadn't even heard the Mexican's words.

"I'm hungry," Rivera said. "Stir up the fire."

Deraux moved toward the low, flickering flame, keenly aware of his situation. If he made a break and managed to elude this crazy Mex in the dark, where would he go and how would he survive without water? Since Rivera had the gun, he could wait by the tanks or stalk him.

Deraux scooped up an armful of brush and several small limbs left by the Indian trackers and threw them on the glowing coals. The dry brush caught and flared up, throwing a glare on Rivera's ruddy face.

"I didn't tell you to light a damned signal fire!" Rivera kicked and scattered some of the blazing branches. The fire died down. He holstered the Colt, then took up a bloody hunk of mule meat, brushed it off, and thrust it on the end of a sharp stick.

"Your English has improved," Deraux said, staring across the fire at Rivera's lean face framed by lank black hair.

Rivera's oily laugh made Deraux's skin crawl. "I tired of playing the stupid, cringing *peón*. Sit down!"

Deraux lowered himself to a cross-legged position on the ground, knowing the Mexican would want him seated, so he couldn't quickly escape or attack, while he ate the meat.

"How did you escape the trackers?" Deraux asked again, more to distract the man from his deadly intentions, than for information.

Rivera inspected the meat on the spit. "Ocano was an ox. I was the wolf," he replied, grinning.

"That tells me nothing." Deraux knew the

Mexican would want to elaborate and boast.

"When you dropped, we figured you for a goner. The big *hombre* took your water and gun."

"Your concern for my welfare overwhelms me."

Rivera's expression hardened in the firelight. "You damned jailbirds forced me to guide you here! Why should I care if the sun shrivels you to raisins?" he snapped. "I knew Ocano would shoot me when I was no more use to him." He paused to pinch off a sliver of meat. It wasn't done to his satisfaction and he thrust it back over the coals. "Even before the sun went down, the ox had drunk all the water and was going down, too." He grinned at his own clever use of words. "To make sure the big *hombre* did not reach the water, I urged him on to the far side of the mountains, walked him an extra five miles until he could walk no more." He laughed his oily laugh. "I told him the water was only a little farther. By the time he saw he'd been suckered, it was too late. He was on his hands and knees, too weak to fight. I hit him in the head with a rock and took the gun belt and canteens."

"Why didn't you shoot him?"

"Too noisy in case anyone was on our trail. And I must save the bullets for later."

"From what I saw, Ocano was still alive," Deraux said.

Rivera shrugged. "No matter. Not my problem now."

"Where are the canteens?"

"That part of my plan went wrong," the Mexican said. "I got a good drink in one of the smaller tanks down there. . . ." He gestured. "Filled the canteens. Heard a horse whinny close by. Jumped for cover just before the Indians came in sight. No time to grab the canteens."

"So the trackers got the canteens . . . and they found Ocano a good ways off . . . ," Deraux said slowly. "They had to know someone else was here."

"I made it look like the ox fell and hit his head on a rock."

"Yuma trackers can read sign. They would know that's not what happened."

Rivera glanced apprehensively around at the darkness that was creeping closer as the fire died.

"But they didn't find you," Deraux continued.

"Ah, *señor,* you forget that I guided you to these tanks. I know these mountains as well as any Indian. There are many places to hide. It would take days to find me." He shrugged. "Those Yumas were lazy. They wanted to eat and drink and take the big *hombre* back for a reward. They did not want to chance being ambushed by a desperate fugitive." He pulled a smoking piece of mule meat off the stick with his fingers and blew on it before placing it gingerly between his teeth. He chewed for a few seconds. "For them, it would be like thrusting their hands under rock ledges in search of rattlesnakes." He grinned, showing tobacco-stained teeth. "They might've killed me, but one or two of them would be dead as well." He took another bite of meat, and chewed with his mouth open. "Ah . . . good!"

Deraux gauged the distance across the low fire. Could he leap onto the damned greaser before he could react? The bone handle of Rivera's knife protruded from his boot top, and he'd witnessed the Mexican's quick reflexes in Yuma. Deraux relaxed, waiting for a better opportunity. Now that he'd satisfied his hunger and thirst, he wanted nothing more than to lie down somewhere and sleep. But it might be the sleep of death if Rivera had his way. He decided to try a different tactic. "Well, we're damned lucky. I guess you'll be headed back to Yuma."

Rivera's eyes narrowed. Deraux didn't know if it was a reaction to the smoke. The

Mexican's mouth was full and he continued chewing without bothering to answer.

"Or travel on with me . . . we'll stand a better chance together." Deraux made an effort to sound friendly, even though the last thing he wanted to do was travel with this man.

"I've got a better idea," Rivera said, wiping his mouth with his sleeve. "I take you back for the reward and get paid for my trouble."

Deraux pretended to ponder this for a moment. "We're marooned on this island without a boat in the middle of the ocean," he said.

"*Hombre,* the sun has made you loco."

"Look around," Deraux said, sweeping his arm at the darkness. "We're surrounded by miles of desert. We can't leave these mountains because we have no canteens or jugs to carry water."

Rivera paused in the middle of cracking a marrowbone. Deraux almost laughed at the stricken look on the Mexican's face. Then the man recovered and sneered. "I will find a way. I'll fill your boots."

"My boots have holes in them."

"Plug them with moss."

"I can't walk barefoot. You'll have to carry me."

"I could just shoot you."

"Then you wouldn't get the reward, unless you produced my body."

"Shut your mouth!"

The Mexican was clearly frustrated. He savagely pounded the bone with a rock.

"I could use some more of that meat," Deraux said blandly.

Rivera ignored him, peering into the hollow of the jagged bone, then raking out some marrow and sucking his finger.

Deraux saw his chance, and slowly rocked backward, sliding out of his cross-legged position.

Rivera put the end of the bone into his mouth.

Deraux pulled his feet under him and sprang. He landed on the smaller man with all his weight, jamming the splintered end of the bone into Rivera's mouth. He heard Rivera gag as they slammed to the ground. Deraux jabbed a short, powerful punch to the jaw, and Rivera's head snapped back. The Mexican reached for his boot knife, but Deraux jammed a knee on the man's wrist, and snatched the knife himself. "I'll slit your damned throat if you move!"

Rivera stopped struggling, his wide eyes rolling back.

Deraux stood up and jerked the wiry man

to his feet, holding the knife point against his ribs. He carefully removed the Colt from Rivera's holster, stepped back a pace, and thumbed back the hammer — praying the weapon was loaded — and slipped the knife under his belt.

But the fight had clearly gone out of Rivera. He spat blood to one side and put a hand to his mouth where the jagged bone had cut him. He mumbled in Spanish under his breath.

"Now that we've settled that," Deraux said, "drop your gun belt to the ground." How was he going to restrain this man? He had no rope or manacles. Then he had an idea. "Let's find that dead mule." He buckled on the gun belt, then took up a blazing stick for light and motioned Rivera to move ahead of him.

The remains of the butchered mule were forty yards away on a slope, downhill from one of the smaller tanks. "Go into the water."

"What?"

"Do what I tell ya. Into the water. Up to your neck."

The Mexican waded carefully into the tank until the water was thigh deep.

"Sit down."

He obeyed.

Deraux holstered the Colt and shoved the blazing stick down for a closer look at the mule, holding his breath against the stench of the bloody offal. Then he pulled the knife from his belt and cut through the large intestine. Pulling out the slippery organ, he cut off a ten-foot section and dragged it to the edge of the tank. "Here. Wash this out. Make sure it's clean, or I'll drown you." He wiped the knife on his pants and shoved it under his belt.

Rivera began splashing and sluicing water through the intestine.

The blazing stick flickered out to a glow and, for several minutes Deraux stood in the dark while Rivera washed the tubular organ.

The splashing stopped. "That's as good as I can do in the dark, *señor*."

"Make damned sure the shit's cleaned out. That's gonna carry your drinking water."

The splashing started again with renewed vigor. Several minutes later, Rivera looped the gut over his shoulder and waded ashore.

When they returned to the fire, Deraux drew the Colt. "Rip the sleeve off your shirt."

Rivera obeyed without question in the face of the loaded pistol.

186

"Tear it into strips and tie one end of that gut tight. Fill it with water from the big tank over there, then tie off the other end."

While Rivera was occupied, Deraux piled the remains of the brush and small branches onto the fire so that it blazed up brightly. The moon had not yet made its appearance.

Rivera dragged the gut, loaded with water, up to the firelight and dropped it. Deraux felt the black eyes darting hate at him. But there was fear in those eyes as well. Deraux knew that, lacking a weapon, the Mex was no match for him. But he also knew that, if his vigilance relaxed, he could wake up dead.

Still holding the gun, Deraux backed down to the tank and waded in, submerging himself into a sitting posture. Several minutes later he waded out and ordered Rivera back in as a means of keeping him semi-restrained until Deraux could slit the sides of his wet boots and pull them off. He threw the ruined socks into the blaze, then examined his feet in the firelight, and dried them. They were blistered and raw, but at least were washed clean of blood and dirt. He cut down the tops of his boots to fashion clumsy, high-top shoes. Then he sliced off one leg of his long underwear to wrap his feet after partially drying it close to the flames. The next time he trekked this desert, he'd be as well prepared as circumstances would allow. He carefully wrapped his sore feet and slipped on the wet shoe boots. His feet felt much better. While Rivera still soaked up to his chin in the tank, Deraux ate more of the roasted haunch. With the sleep he'd had, along with the food and water, his strength was restored, although he could still use several more hours of rest.

But that could wait. They'd move out tonight, pointing north by east, to intersect the Gila Road, miles away. He didn't care if the trackers saw the fire from several miles out. If the Yumas decided to return and add to their prisoners, Deraux and Rivera would be long gone. Traveling at night would avoid the worst heat, would keep the Indians from spotting them on the open desert, and would also solve Deraux's problem of how to restrain the wily Mexican.

He pointed the gun at the tank. "All right . . . out!" He motioned with the pistol. "If you haven't soaked the stink off by now, I can travel upwind of you. Loop that water gut over your shoulder and let's move out."

CHAPTER ELEVEN

July 31, 1878
Northeast of Yuma,
Arizona Territory

It took the better part of a week for the peace of the desert to seep back into Daniel Mora's soul.

From Yuma, he led his new burro, Kismet, north, along the east side of the Colorado River. For two days he endured the intense heat of midsummer before reverting to his practice of resting during the hottest part of the day, then setting out at sunset and traveling well past dark when the moon was high. He would then camp for a few hours of sleep, only to rise an hour before dawn to move until the morning sun grew too hot for comfort.

The third morning he filled his canteens and two small water kegs and struck away from the river, toward the Chocolate Mountains. These desert ranges were neither as high nor as wooded as the Catalinas near Tucson. And they were definitely not as cool. But tantalizing traces of gold and silver had been discovered in their remote cañons and outcroppings — if one could endure the heat, the lack of water, and somehow avoid or fend off the Apaches. Mora had no doubt this part of the territory would eventually be riddled with producing mines, many of them very rich.

The heat didn't bother him, as long as he took a few precautions for himself and his animal. He was careful to be sure his burro wasn't overloaded, and drank sufficient water from the two wooden kegs the animal carried. Kismet was not human company, but that wasn't necessarily bad. He'd always possessed an instinctive rapport with animals of whatever species, and was comfortable with only the burro. It wasn't long before he recognized Kismet's various moods — when she was content, or hungry, or ready to break free and go wandering. She would eat nearly any kind of vegetation that wasn't too thorny.

As he led the docile burro up a shallow valley, he pondered her practical uses as beast of burden, a sentry who would bray loudly at the approach of animal or man, and a killer of snakes. For Mora, these traits made the burro nearly perfect as a traveling companion.

Just as before his Sierra Madre adventure, he felt no urgency in his quest for gold. He had the rest of his life — however long that might be. Gold was only a means of subsistence. Yet he still owed Lila Strunk the money she'd given him for his grubstake. This was the only obligation he felt. He had an inkling that Lila cared for him as a possible soul mate and husband. She would doubtless make a fine wife, but he was not in the market for a wife, even if he'd been free to marry. He still had a wife in San Francisco. At least, he presumed she still lived. He'd had no word of her death, and there was always someone who'd seek you out with news like that.

Mora pulled up to take a breather and to adjust the pack saddle. The morning sun rose higher, stoking the furnace of the sere mountains. Others found this country forbidding, but he felt at home in the folds and ridges of the rocky landscape. True, he was a stranger wandering a strange land, and would never have a true home until he laid his bones in the dust for the last time, his spirit traveling on to explore whatever lay beyond. But that didn't concern him as he hunkered in the scant shade of his animal to swig lukewarm water from his canteen. He wondered if anyone would find and bury his remains. In this extremely dry atmosphere, it wouldn't take many weeks before his body would look like an unwrapped, desiccated mummy, similar to the Apache he'd seen hanging from the cross along the Gila Road. He was saved from further morbid thoughts when a tiny lizard paused, looked quizzically at him before darting into the shade of a mesquite.

He chuckled, then stood and poured water into his new felt hat. He offered a drink to Kismet who drank greedily. "Atta girl." He rubbed her nose and long ears as she nuzzled his pockets for a possible treat.

In spite of his contentment, a tiny uneasy feeling tugged at his innards. He paid little attention to it, not being so naïve as to think he would ever find perfect happiness in this life. There were always mice in the corncrib, flies on the apple pie, *cholera morbis* in the belly, or a shrewish wife to find fault.

Most men and women were more sociable than he, and couldn't stand the silence of the recluse. He had no such attachments to others of his kind. A little human company went a long way. He'd discovered the hard way that he couldn't put trust in people. He supposed he had faults that irritated others, but now they didn't have to put up with him, either.

Until his water ran low, he prospected for several days in both the Chocolate Mountains and the Castle Dome district to the east, picking up float, chipping off promising rock samples, numbering small rocks he dropped into a canvas bag, and penciling their numbers and approximate locations into a notebook.

One clear morning before dawn, he and Kismet started toward the village of Castle Dome Landing, on the Colorado, to replenish water and supplies and to visit the assayer. Guiding himself by the sun and stars, Mora made his crooked way through the desert and low mountains. Twice he spotted evidence of claims being worked. In each instance, he stopped some distance away to observe through his field glasses. At the first, no one was around, but a shaft was surmounted by a windlass and hoist, with a pile of spoil to one side. A small operation that had not proved up, or the miners had been run off or killed by Indians, he guessed. The following day, about sunset, he spied a new-looking head frame overtop another shaft. He stopped on a hill upwind to keep Kismet from braying at the smell of the mules that plodded around the primitive arrastre, crushing ore. This larger operation had the appearance of something more profitable. Through the twin lenses of his field glasses, he saw three men moving around. Mora wondered if they were mining gold or silver or copper. He didn't plan to go down and inquire. He was irritated that mines and miners were becoming more numerous in the Castle Dome district. The remote mountains, it seemed, were filling up. Before long, the sound of steam engines and the thunderous pounding of stamp mills would be fouling the silence, echoing off the ancient boulders and rock walls. Then he smiled to himself. No, that wouldn't happen unless a source of water were discovered. The crushed ore would still have to be hauled by wagon or mule back to the river.

The next morning, Mora was startled awake by Kismet's loud braying. He sprang up and silenced her, then kicked dirt on the remaining coals of his campfire. He wanted no part of whatever had alerted her. He quickly strapped on her pack saddle, slipped off the hobbles, and took up his rifle and lead rope, cat-footing down the cañon while a rosy dawn lighted the eastern horizon. A few minutes later a chill crawled up his back. He clamped a hand over Kismet's nose and watched as a half dozen Indians rode in loose single file against the skyline, heading east, over a ridge and out of his sight. If they'd heard his burro, they ignored the sound, intent on some destination of their own. Possibly they attributed the noise to one of the wild burros that roamed these hills.

By sunset that evening, he was watering his burro among the rushes in a backwater of the Colorado. He'd left ore samples with the assayer, who'd promised to have the results the next morning. Mora hoped there was enough gold in the samples to pay the assayer, with a little left over. He was out of cash. This lack of funds killed his temptation to go to the saloon for a couple of beers. That would have to wait. For now, he filled his water kegs and canteens, bathed and washed his clothing in the water among the thick rushes, then dried off by a campfire a half mile outside Castle Dome Landing.

Content with the company of his burro, Mora went to bed after a supper of jerked beef and water, as happy as he'd ever been.

"These specimens don't have enough of anything to bother with," the bearded assayer said, nudging the rock samples aside

195

with calloused, blackened fingers. He glanced at Mora over his glasses. "Now, these show maybe . . . forty dollars of gold to the ton, with some traces of copper and silver."

"Three ounces of pure metal in two thousand pounds of rock." Mora grinned ruefully at the absurdity. "Reckon I'll have to train my eyes a little better." He took a deep breath, the scorched smell of the assayer's fire burning his nostrils.

The assayer grunted his assent. "These last two, on the other hand, show more promise than I've seen in some time. He held them to the sunlight by the window. "See those threads of gold veining the quartz? It goes at least two thousand to the ton. The other one is even richer . . . maybe three thousand."

Mora's heart leaped and he did some quick mental calculations. An average of ten or eleven pounds of pure gold to each ton of rock. He knew this was only a small sample. The gold it contained could very likely dwindle off to nothing a few inches either side of where he'd broken off the specimen.

"Definitely worth pursuing," the assayer said, handing over the two samples. He was strictly business, showing no more emotion than a man who earned his keep tasting whiskey at a distillery.

"Keep one of these for your work," Mora said.

"Thanks."

"Is the other one rich enough to pay for a few supplies?"

The assayer nodded. "Sure is, if Harkness over at the General Store still accepts gold ore in place of specie. He'll have to have it smelted to extract the exact weight and value." The assayer smiled for the first time. "I'd sure as hell take it. But the most valuable thing you have here is the knowledge of where it came from."

Mora forced a smile as he shoved the ore sample into his pants pocket. He'd have to consult his notebook, but even then his notations were rather vague, since distinguishable landmarks were lacking. Most of those cañons and ridges looked much alike.

At the General Store he bought dried beans, cornmeal, bacon, salve for Kismet's back, jerked beef, canned tomatoes, and matches. The clerk apparently had been told to accept likely looking ore or nuggets, and the young man seemed unusually curious, trying to find out where the ore had come from. But Mora was uncommunicative, and departed shortly, leading Kismet away from the small town, away from the river and back toward the mountains. He kept a sharp eye on his back trail in case anyone had decided to follow him. The only thing bad about finding gold was that it was worthless unless traded for something — traded to other men who could be wily, greedy, even murderous.

He made camp early that evening, then rose before dawn next day to lead his burro on a circuitous route, doubling back on himself, crossing slabs of solid rock where the only track he could leave might be a scratch from an iron horseshoe. For two more days, he kept up his twisting, turning course to discourage or confuse any would-be followers. He was probably paranoid, but better safe than dead, he reasoned. He needed to take care to avoid becoming as addled by fear and the sun as other solitary prospectors he'd heard about.

Finally he reached the area of the Castle Dome Mountains where he thought he'd collected the rich samples. Footsore and weary, he made camp on a level ledge of rock commanding a view to the south and west. He collected enough dead wood and brush to build a fire and let it burn down to coals before sunset so no flame could be seen after dark. He filled a small pot with frijoles and buried them in the embers of the campfire, then sat down to smoke his pipe and enjoy the last, lingering rays of the summer sun as the world turned away toward night. A perfect silence rang in his ears; it was hard to realize he was seated on a planet spinning several thousand miles an hour.

A light breeze sprang up to stir the sluggish air, while the rocks around him still gave off the heat of the sun's baking. Dusk slid away to darkness. Before moonrise, the night sky was clear and sparkling with myriad stars and planets, none of which he could name beyond the North Star and the Big Dipper. He pondered incomprehensible infinity. Being too absorbed in the here and now, he'd never thought much about the vast realm of outer space. Letting his gaze wander over the millions of tiny points of light, he sank into the immeasurable distance — and felt like a tiny grain of sand on the earth. At least studying the night sky put the puny activities of man in perspective. Mora could understand how many primitive tribes, faced with the awesome grandeur of the heavenly planets, worshipped these bodies as all-powerful and life-giving forces.

The moon began to rise, silvering the

landscape. In the silence of his mind, Mora could hear the beginning notes of the "Moonlight" Sonata, the lovely piece he'd been privileged to enjoy more than once in a San Francisco concert hall. Yet even the beauty of this Beethoven composition was hardly as impressive as the real thing.

He inhaled the fresh fragrance of the desert vegetation. At this moment, the wealthiest man in America possessed no more than he. He prayed for a stronger faith in God, for complete confidence in the personal Supreme Being who cared about Daniel Mora and all the rest of creation. Even though he'd bumbled into a few box cañons along the way, he was reasonably satisfied most of his major decisions had been correct. The faint unease that troubled him might only be a longing for the perfect happiness of heaven.

This reflection was the closest he'd come to consciously praying in weeks, he thought as he removed the lid from the beans, smelled the delicious aroma, and prepared to eat.

The sun was nearly overhead the next day when he paused to drink from his canteen. He'd resolved to take shelter during the hottest hours, but was close to relocating the place where he'd taken the rich samples and didn't want to stop until he found it.

He watered Kismet, then, using his shirt tail, wiped the dust from the lenses of his green-tinted glasses. Looking backward and forward along the narrow cañon, he strove to orient himself. He no longer had the two samples to compare with the rock outcroppings, but his memory for land forms and details stood him in good stead. He ruffled the pages of his small notebook and read that a steep, rocky ridge jutted up on the west side of the cañon, while a spire of rock was visible 100 yards farther to the north. This had to be the place. He tethered Kismet to a rock in the shade of an overhanging ledge. The windless air was stifling in the narrow defile as he began his climb up to the left. The sun was like a heavy blanket pressing down on him, making every labored step more of an effort.

After climbing twenty feet, he paused to catch his breath and look for handholds and footholds in the broken rock ledges farther up. The rock burned his callused hands even through the worn leather gloves. He tilted his head back and the sun smote his face beneath the hat brim. Just another dozen feet or so. That's where he'd taken the samples; he was almost certain of it. He started his climb once more.

Finally reaching the level ledge, he found the sharp edge of fractured rock where scratches from his hammer were still visible. Peering closely at the outcropping, he worked his way along, noting only one more tiny trace of gold. If he didn't see anything more promising than this in the amber-colored rock, he'd knock off and hunker down somewhere until later when he'd come back and try again. Perhaps sunlight at a lower angle would reveal something.

He went to his hands and knees and looked closely where a seam of stained rock and quartz seemed to mingle. Then he felt a tiny whiff of cool air, and jerked back, startled. He yanked off a glove and put his hand to the crack. The air was cooler, as if emanating from a cave. The crack was where several rocks had slid down to block an opening in the seamed and weathered face of the mountain. He pulled at the smaller rocks and they fell away, crashing down below him in a cloud of dust. He forced aside two more pan-size slabs until he had an opening large enough to crawl into. The cool air felt wonderful on his face as he went to his hands and knees and worked his way inside, praying there were no reptiles lying in the sheltered darkness. Ten feet from the entrance, he was able to stand up. He paused until his eyes adjusted to the gloom. Light was not only coming from the entrance he'd uncovered, but also from a ray of noon sun slanting down through a crack twenty feet above. It shone on a mossy wall of rock where a tiny trickle glistened.

"Water! By God!" He moved toward it when his desert moccasins scuffed against something that rattled across the floor. He jumped aside with a thrill of fear, his heart pounding. He'd kicked a skeleton; a mummified skull grinned at him in the shaft of overhead light. He swallowed his heart that had jumped into his throat, then bent to examine the grisly discovery. There was not one body, but two. Both had been mummified by the dry heat, brown skin stretching over skulls that retained a fringe of hair, eye sockets filled with the dust of decay, tips of noses gone, teeth showing in macabre grins through gaps where the lips had vanished. Withered, skeletal hands were covered with parchment-like skin, as were bony feet still clutched in dry sandals, their leather straps scarred by the gnawing of rats. The crowns of both skulls were broken.

But what filled him with wonder was the sight of their clothing. Each body wore a hooded brown robe and a rope waist cinch

— the dress of Franciscan friars.

Mora knelt and listened to the silence of centuries. How long had these men lain here undisturbed? They both showed signs of violent death. They might have died five years ago, or fifty, or 150. There was no way he could tell. The buckles on the sandals were of an unfamiliar design, and the coarse cloth looked to be hand woven. But what were they doing here? Had they crawled into this cleft to escape wild animals, or the heat, or a flash flood, or the Indians? Had they been killed by a cave-in? There were no rocks of any size lying about that would account for the crushed skulls.

When he'd calmed down, he rose and proceeded to examine the rest of the small cave. The shaft of sunlight picked out something near the floor. He stooped to look — and caught his breath. There, imbedded in the base of the wall, was coarse sponge gold, entwined and laced through white quartz rock. The gold was nearly pure, and there was a lot of it. From the looks of the marks, some of it had been hacked away. Was this what the priests had been after? No telling how far the two-foot wide vein extended into the rock. But there was enough within sight to make him a wealthy man. His heart pounded with the thrill of it.

He rocked back on his heels and studied the softly gleaming metal. The enormity of his discovery gradually settled on him — and with it settled the weight of a ponderous depression.

CHAPTER TWELVE

Daniel Mora wasn't aware how long he hunkered, mesmerized, before the golden treasure. Time ceased and he seemed suspended in some eerily lighted shrine where the riches of the world lay before him for the taking. Possibilities, implications, and problems whirled through his mind faster than he could focus on them.

His trance was finally broken when the sunlight slid away from the dull gleam in the white quartz. He blinked, rubbed his eyes, then rose and moved from the wall. His gaze fell on the withered, brown-robed sentinels of the treasure. How ironic that these Franciscans, who'd taken a vow of poverty, would have ended their days beside all this worldly wealth — if, in fact, they were actually killed here. He had no doubt they'd been murdered, their deaths somehow connected to this gold. He also suspected their killers had long since turned to dust as well.

His mind began to function clearly once more. He took the small hammer from his belt and, with a few deft strokes, knocked off several chips of rotten quartz, surprised at how soft the pure gold was. The earth yielded up her riches without a struggle, but this ready access made Mora nervous. It shouldn't be this easy. That was not in the nature of things. Something was amiss. It was like struggling to push open a heavy door, only to have it unexpectedly fly open, causing him to fall inside.

He pulled an empty rawhide bag from under his belt and began to fill it with samples. Yet these were not really ore samples. They were about half to two-thirds pure gold intertwined with some white quartz. He whistled softly at its richness.

Twice he thought he heard a noise outside and paused to listen, holding his breath. Once he even put the bag down and crawled carefully back through the narrow entrance, slipped on his green glasses, and looked around. Nothing. Everything was hot and still. The small desert animals and birds had all gone to their burrows or nests to shelter from the blasting early afternoon sun. From the ledge he could see Kismet, her tail swishing at flies as the patient burrow awaited his return in the shade of the narrow cañon below. Mora crawled back inside, his heart thumping. He was perspiring, even in the slightly cooler, musty atmosphere. The gold was already working on his nerves. He'd left his carbine on the pack saddle, never anticipating having to defend himself. He wished he had a small pistol that would be easy to carry. Anyone could easily slip up, unseen, from the outside and trap him in this cleft — a cleft that was almost a cave formed by the tilting of giant slabs of rock.

Pulling the drawstring tight, he hefted the rawhide bag and was amazed at its weight. He tied it to his belt, then went to examine the moisture on the nearby rock. It was only a tiny seepage that had aided the formation of moss. It was water, all right, but not enough to get a decent drink if a man stood here for a week and sponged off every drop.

Needing fresh air, he turned toward the entrance. Even if it was hotter outside, claustrophobia had begun to claw at his throat. This golden tomb seemed to be suffocating him.

Suddenly he remembered he had to stake a claim, if this was to be his. Although the vein showed evidence of having been worked, it might have been done by Indians or early missionaries. To hold a claim that had been staked and filed on, the law required that a miner do some minimal assessment work. It was evident no activity had taken place here in many years, probably even decades. He collected and formed a pile of the small rocks that littered the floor and took out his notebook and pencil. Standing in the narrow beam of overhead light, he wrote his name and the date and the statement that he, Daniel Mora, was claiming all the gold within this cave as his, along with all the gold the exposed vein might contain. Claiming the entire vein, no matter where it might lead was probably not strictly legal, but it would have to do until he got to the recorder's office to file. In most alluvial claims on creeks and rivers, there was a limit on the number of feet a claim could extend along the waterway, as well as from rimrock to rimrock on either side. Dating and signing the page, he tore it from his notebook and tucked it under the top rock in the pyramid-shaped pile.

What about these two bodies? Should he bury them in the sand outside? If they were found here, along with his name, someone might accuse him of murder. He pondered the situation and decided to leave the two dead priests where they were. If anyone else wandered in here, maybe the sight would distract them so they wouldn't see the gold vein. And it wouldn't hurt to disguise the vein.

He crawled back outside, slipping and sliding down to the floor of the narrow cañon, and retrieved his shovel from the burro. He dug up two small mesquite bushes, along with some dirt around their bases, then laboriously climbed back up to the ledge, spilling some of the dirt from the shovel into his own face. He made his way inside the cleft. The dirt he mixed with what little moisture and moss he could get from the seepage in the wall, then smeared the resulting mud on the exposed gold and white quartz. The mesquite he placed at the base of the wall in front of the gold, then stepped back to review his handiwork. Even in the better light of a lantern, the vein would not be noticeable, unless one were looking for it.

Wearing his work gloves, he returned the displaced skull to the body of the mummy, then, using a small branch of the mesquite, brushed out his tracks and scuff marks in the dust as he crawled backward out the low entrance. He'd left no tracks on the ledge or the jumbled scree. He wrestled a rock over the opening he'd uncovered. An expert tracker might be able to tell someone had climbed up and down here, but he felt relatively secure no one would come looking.

He returned to Kismet, uncorked one of the small water kegs, and poured his hat full for her to drink. Then replacing the cool, wet hat, he drank from his canteen.

"Well, gal, you and I are rich," he said quietly, rubbing her velvety nose. She nuzzled his hand. "Nothing for you just now, but I've got enough in this sack to buy anything you want." Her soft brown eyes showed not a trace of avarice, and he laughed aloud. "I used to think I was as immune to money as you are, but now I'm not so sure." He grew solemn, listening to the midday stillness and wondering at his own reaction to the find. "I'll let you carry this." He removed the heavy rawhide sack from his belt and tied it out of sight under the blankets on the burro's pack saddle.

He took the rope and led the burro out into the fierce sun, intent on finding a place to shelter for the next three or four hours. Two miles away, he pulled off the pack saddle in the shade of a *palo verde,* unrolled his blanket on the ground, and stretched out. He tied the burro on a long lead, still unsure if she might take it into her head to go wandering. And he couldn't afford to lose her. He lay down to rest, but placed the Marlin beside him in an unusual gesture of self-defense.

By the time shadows were growing long, Mora had resaddled Kismet and was leading her toward the retreating sun. His first order of business was to settle his debt to Lila Strunk. Along the way, he would stop in Yuma and record his claim. How could he do this without calling attention to his find, and either starting a stampede or putting himself in danger? He would figure that out as he went along. In the two years he'd been a lone prospector, he'd never found anything rich enough to file on. His had been merely a subsistence existence, picking up promising-looking float here and there, chipping off rock samples that contained enough gold to trade for a few supplies. Should he hire the smelter at Castle Dome Landing to reduce his gold to one small ingot of pure metal? No. That would be costly. The smelter was set up to deal with large amounts of ore that were already being brought down by mule train from the commercial mines in the region. Gold as pure as his samples would surely bring comment. Word would leak out, and he would be followed, questioned, maybe even threatened to reveal the location of the ore. Blessings of any kind did not come in unadulterated form, he realized. He'd just use his knife point to dig out a few small nuggets from the quartz to trade for stage fare, food, and a livery stable bill for Kismet while he returned to Sand Tank station.

The thought of seeing Lila again after less than three weeks gladdened his heart. Perhaps he wasn't the natural-born hermit he'd imagined. But Lila was different. She was easy to talk to, relaxing to be around. What made her so appealing? She'd evidently been pretty in her youth, but could hardly be considered so now. She hadn't become embittered by hardship. On the contrary, she still had an easy laugh, along with a level head and common sense. After some thought, he finally focused on the quality that set her apart from other women, and most men, he'd known — she was not judgmental. In the case of her Mexican hostler, Rivera, she'd been forced to judge. She'd hired him out of desperation, but feared him and fired him as soon as Quanto came on the scene to fill the job. Mora had seen no evidence she tried to change others into what she thought they should be. Regardless of what private thoughts she entertained, she came across as a woman who accepted others at face value, never ascribing ulterior motives to their actions.

He imagined what she would say, how she would react when he poured out the gold in front of her, repaying her generosity and trust many times over for the grubstake she'd provided from her own meager savings. He smiled at the thought of her surprise and wonder, at her joy over his good fortune.

That night, sitting cross-legged by his campfire, he held chunks of the rich ore and gouged out tiny pieces of gold onto his blanket — pieces small enough they weren't likely to draw any undue curiosity. These might be tiny flakes and nuggets any desert rat could have raked up from a gravelly arroyo.

The heat was so intense, Mora took a leisurely two more days to reach Castle Dome Landing. He remained grubby and dusty and unshaven to divert suspicion from any observer that he might have more than 10¢ and a chew of Wedding Cake plug in his pockets.

Fortunately the stage company had run a branch line north from Yuma, so he wouldn't have to walk any farther. He bought a round trip ticket to Sand Tank station at the stage office while pretending to hoard the tiny nuggets he used to pay for it.

Then he led Kismet to the town's lone livery. "Put 'er up with good feed and a rubdown. Keep her exercised. I'll be gone about ten days to two weeks. I'll stow my pack saddle and gear in your tack room."

"Right." The barrel-bellied liveryman gave him a slight smirk that said as loudly as words: "If you don't show up again, or can't pay, I'll have me a good animal here."

Mora fished out three small nuggets, estimated their weight in his hand at two ounces, and dropped them into the merchant's outstretched palm.

"Yes, sir! Anything else, sir?" The fat man's eyes bugged and he became subservient at once.

Mora stroked the burro's neck in farewell and went off quickly to board the stage that was leaving in a half hour. Perhaps it wasn't healthy to become so attached to animals, but Kismet was his constant, and only, companion. He'd come to value and depend on her company. It had been that way with Atlas, his first burro. They each had different personalities, but he never had to be on his guard around a burro as he did around humans. A burro was more predictable. He'd miss her.

Early that morning, Mora had taken pains to wrap the rawhide ore sack inside his blanket and ground cover, lacing the roll securely at both ends. The rolled bundle he carried like a grip by way of a rope handle. In spite of the driver's instructions to stow it, along with his rifle, in the boot, he kept both inside the coach. For one thing, he didn't want anyone to notice how heavy the roll was for its size. He hated that such precautions were necessary, but regretted even more that he now looked on every stranger with suspicion. The gold was definitely having its affect on him, and he'd acquired it only three days before.

The four men who were to share the stage on its thirty-mile run to Yuma introduced themselves as soon as they all boarded.

Mora had offered his hand to each of the other three, saying: "Daniel Mora, prospector."

A young second lieutenant, named Jim Briscoe, was traveling from his upriver post at Ehrenberg to Fort Yuma.

"Ned Weems. I sell the finest liquors made," a short, rotund man said, offering his sweaty palm.

"P.J. Edwards," the last man said, settling into his seat next to Mora and removing his hat to reveal a severely balding pate. "I represent some mining interests." He didn't offer to shake hands.

"Yeeehaww!" A whip cracked, and the stage jerked into motion.

"Hope the driver can convey all that energy to those mules," Lieutenant Briscoe said with a smile. Somehow, the officer still looked neat and fresh in his blue uniform.

Within a quarter mile, the stage began to dip and sway and bounce, throwing them from one side to the other.

"Gawd damn!" The red-faced whiskey drummer opposite Mora grabbed for the hanging strap as a heavy lurch flung him against the paneled side. "If that driver's tryin' to hit every pothole and rut 'tween here and Yuma, he's doing a dang' good job of it!"

Mora, who was facing rearward, wanted to tell Weems that he should be glad he wasn't walking, as he himself had been doing for many days. But he was long past telling others what to do or say. Besides, as he studied the man's flushed face and the spidery tracing of tiny veins in the chubby cheeks, he felt pity for Ned Weems, out on the road trying to make a living selling whiskey, bourbon, rye, Scotch, and various other hard liquors. The drummer propped his feet on his wooden sample case and, with his free hand, yanked loose his maroon cravat. He'd already doffed his waistcoat, and the striped shirt clung to him in sweaty patches. The hot wind puffed in the open windows, carrying a fine layer of dust.

It was almost with a sense of guilt that Mora reflected on the fortune he'd found. Although he looked grubbier than any of the other three, he was probably richer than any man in, or atop, the coach. In fact, he could probably buy this stagecoach line, with plenty left over for a mansion or two and some first-class world travel. It wasn't pride or a feeling of superiority that made him feel far removed from these men who pursued jobs and professions to earn their living; it was more a feeling of unreality. He'd probably wake up on his blanket shortly, with Kismet nearby, and realize this was only some crazy dream. Yet, he knew it wasn't. As a child, he and his friends had sometimes played the game: "What would you do if you had a million dollars?" Then followed the wildest schemes and plans and castles in the air as each boy tried to stretch his imagination and outdo the others in spending this extravagant, imaginary fortune.

Mora took a deep breath and looked out at the sun's brilliant reflection skipping along the surface of the Colorado River. Now he didn't have to pretend. He actually possessed such wealth, and, if that vein was as rich as it appeared, he was likely worth more than the million dollars they'd conjured up as children.

Yet, he couldn't get too excited about the find. This reality might vanish in a puff of smoke when he reached the recorder's office and found out the rich vein already belonged to someone else. But he strongly suspected this was not the case. Someone obviously had known about the ore in the past, since the vein showed signs of having been worked. Perhaps it was Indians. But the presence of the long-dead bodies, the undisturbed dust and rat droppings all indicated this was no recent claim or a mine currently being worked.

For several minutes, they rode in silence. Then Weems retrieved his folded coat and fished out a fat cigar. "Since there are no ladies present, would you gents care for a smoke?"

They all declined, and Weems proceeded to cup a match away from the breeze long enough to light up. "Ahhh . . . nothing like a good cigar to make a man feel better," he sighed, blowing out a cloud of fragrant white smoke. "Probably one of three things in life worth bothering about." He appeared disappointed that no one asked him to name the other two.

Mora was not inclined to strike up conversations with strangers, but something had been eating at the back of his mind. He propped one ankle across his knee to help support the bedroll in his lap, and glanced sideways at P.J. Edwards. "I'm surprised there's not a recording clerk in Castle Dome Landing," he remarked.

"To file claims?"

"Yes."

"When the Castle Dome mining district was organized about fourteen years ago, the first recorder was Mister Ehrenberg at La Paz."

"The same Ehrenberg the town's named after?"

"So I'm told. I wasn't here then, but some time later the job was turned over to the county court clerk in Yuma." The taciturn Edwards said no more.

"You've struck something up in those hills, Mora?" Lieutenant Briscoe asked with a smile.

"Do I look like I've struck anything?" Mora asked. "I'm thinking ahead, in case. Have you ever known a prospector who didn't think he was going to strike the mother lode tomorrow?"

"I've never met an honest-to-goodness prospector before," Lieutenant Briscoe said. "But I suppose a man has to have faith, or he'd wouldn't keep at it."

"For me, it's a way of life. Don't know what I'd do if I actually struck it rich," Mora said, reflecting on the veracity of his statement.

The lieutenant and Weems chuckled. Edwards, pokerfaced, stared straight ahead, apparently lost in thought.

Mora had an idea of pumping Edwards for more information about the procedure for recording a claim, the cost, the maximum size, and other details he'd been wondering about. But Edwards didn't appear inclined to talk, and Mora didn't want to excite any suspicions that he was doing more than just making conversation.

The shadows were stretching down the streets of Yuma when the stage rolled to a stop. The passengers climbed out and went their separate ways.

Mora lugged his heavy bedroll and rifle to the nearest decent-looking hotel and checked in, paying in advance for one night with a tiny gold nugget. The hotel clerk kept a set of gold scales behind the counter for such customers, as did several of the saloons in town. Mora would later consider smelting his gold, and perhaps converting it to coin or paper money at some bank. For now, he'd keep his head down and spend tiny flakes and grains of the precious metal as he went.

Three hours later, he lighted the lamp on the bedside washstand and gazed at himself in the mirror. He'd invested in a shave and haircut, a long soak in a hot tub at a Chinese bathhouse, and some new clothing from the mercantile. Feeling like a new man, he'd filled up with a well-done antelope steak, potatoes, and fresh bread at the best restaurant he could find. He rubbed his clean, smooth jaw and grinned at himself in the glass.

"There *are* some good things to be said about civilization," he muttered aloud. "I even smell good."

He yawned mightily and turned toward the bed. After sleeping on the hard ground, this cotton tick mattress would feel like a cloud.

CHAPTER THIRTEEN

"Your name?" The thin clerk in the white shirt and black vest looked over his reading glasses, pen poised above a thick ledger on the wide counter top.

"Daniel Mora. That's M-O-R-A."

The clerk's pen scratched across the page.

"The name of the claim you wish to register?"

"Uh . . . it has to have a name?"

"It's customary, especially if you have more than one, or if the property is later transferred."

"Sold, you mean?"

"Sold, given away, willed . . . transferred in some manner."

"Umm . . . I'll call it the Saint Francis."

The clerk duly recorded it, and re-dipped his steel pen. "How big?"

"What?"

"The dimensions of this claim."

"As big as the law allows."

"Is it located on a stream?"

"No. In a higher elevation. A vein."

"The maximum for a vein of ore is three hundred feet from point of origin, including any branches or spurs," the clerk recited in a bored tone.

"The point of origin is where I staked it?"

"That's correct."

"Good. That'll do." Mora snorted at the tone of this condescending, insipid clerk. He'd dealt with his share of them in the Department of the Interior.

Mora's new cotton shirt was beginning to itch in the morning heat, and he wanted to get this over with, pay his $2 fee, and escape into the fresh air outside. The stuffy office with the tall windows smelled faintly of cigar smoke.

"To retain the claim, you must work it at least four days a month,"

"Who's going to check?" Mora grinned.

The clerk stared at him as if he'd lost his mind. After a slight hesitation, the clerk said: "I trust you brought a sample of the ore."

Mora fished out a chunk half the size of a coffee cup. It was mostly quartz.

The clerk glanced at it, then set it to one side.

"You going to keep it?"

"Yes. It becomes part of the record on file for comparison with other samples in case the claim is disputed."

"That happen often?"

"More than you'd think." The clerk made another notation. "Now, where is this Saint Francis claim located?"

"In the Castle Dome Mining District."

"You must be more specific." He swiveled his tall stool, pulled open a wide, flat drawer from a cabinet behind him, withdrew a large-scale map, and spread it on the counter. "Locate it for me on this."

Mora studied the detailed topographic map of the Castle Dome District. Without tracing anything with a finger, he used only his eyes to orient himself. He was not accustomed to viewing a layout from an overhead perspective, and found it difficult. Finally he thought he could follow his own route from the river to the approximate location of his newly named Saint Francis claim. "Not real sure, but. . . ."

The clerk drew a deep breath and tapped the steel nib of his pen impatiently on the flip-top ink well. He glanced over his reading glasses at the wall clock, then at the next customer seated nearby, holding a sheaf of papers. "I also need a physical description of the landscape," the clerk snapped.

Mora continued to scan the map. "What for?"

"In order to set this claim apart, to be sure it is not confused with any other, you must give me one or more identifiable land- marks," the clerk said, as if instructing a dull-witted child.

Mora looked up. He was fairly sure he could pinpoint his discovery location now. "Is this information public record?"

"Of course."

"There's no privacy, then, no protection from claim-jumpers . . . except for this?" He hefted his carbine that rested against his bedroll.

"If it's properly recorded, you have the force of law and the courts on your side in any legal dispute."

" 'The force of law and the courts,' " Mora repeated in a monotone, staring vacantly at the map, visions of his own hon- est career being crushed by that same authority. He reached over and picked up his chunk of ore. "Sorry I bothered you. Thanks for your time."

"What? You're not going to register your claim?"

Mora picked up his bedroll and rifle and was halfway to the door when the heavy ledger slammed behind him, cutting off a disgusted comment by the clerk.

During the hot, dusty trip along the Gila Road to Sand Tank station, Mora paid little attention to his surroundings. He'd stowed his Marlin in the boot since there wasn't much elbow room inside the bouncing, swaying coach he shared with six others — a woman with an infant, two rough-looking civilians, a well-dressed man, and a lean, weathered man in buckskins.

The stage departed at daybreak and stopped to change teams at isolated swing stations about twenty miles apart.

During the lunch stop, Mora chose to decline the greasy offerings served up to the passengers. He poured himself a cup of coffee and strolled outside the stifling adobe building, preoccupied with thoughts of his new gold claim. *Is it a mistake not to register it?* He sipped the scalding brew, squinting over the lip of his cup at the parched, duncolored landscape surrounding him. *No.* He had not made a mistake, he decided, thrusting all doubt aside. What was done, was done, and he'd live with it. As of now, he was doubtless the only living human who knew of this rich vein.

A withering noon wind kicked up dust, and he paced to the lee side of the building where he slipped the twisted rope from his shoulder, lowering his bedroll to the ground. The ore was heavy. For the first time since leaving San Francisco in near despair two years earlier, he gave serious thought to taking as much of the gold as he could carry and moving to a more civilized part of the country where he could afford a life of leisure — possibly develop some new interests. A tempting thought, but, deep down, he knew it was only a daydream. Idle luxury was not for him. Why should he mark time until he died just because he had enough wealth to live without working? He'd come to think of himself as a nomad, a desert rat. There was something simple and unchanging about the desert that appealed to him. If the summer heat became unbearable, he could migrate to the high country to the north for a few months until the balmy winter returned to the Gila valley.

Mora was aware the outdoor life and freedom from artificial concerns had made him as fit and lean and content as he'd ever been. He also realized he was closing in on sixty and his stamina was beginning to erode. Small, telltale signs of aging were making themselves known. He instinctively husbanded his strength. Soon he might have to trade his burro for a mule he could ride.

For now, he'd travel as lightly as possible. With this in mind, he'd bought a pistol that morning in a Yuma hardware store. It was a Smith & Wesson new model number three, in .38 caliber. It retained the saw-handle grip of the Russian model, was nickel-plated, and had a five-inch barrel. All in all, a nice weapon, without excess weight or length, but powerful enough for defense and quick to reload with the top-break action.

It was a shame he had to carry a gun at all, except for hunting, but he had no illusions about the lure of the yellow metal. Many men out there would doubtless kill him for much less than he was carrying in his bedroll at this moment. Would the claim marker of rocks and his handwritten note be enough to deter anyone who happened upon it? Not for a second. But the location was so remote, the chances of someone discovering the vein were minimal. Yet, he'd found it, so someone else surely could, especially since the Castle Dome mountains were being explored by more and more prospectors. The well-trained eye of some geologist brought in by mining interests might spot the likely-looking formation or rock strata and follow it up to the St. Francis. If a prospector noticed the rocks at the entrance had been disturbed, found the opening, and crawled inside, would he discover the vein beneath the dirt and the dead mesquite he'd used to disguise it? The claim marker he'd made would be a dead giveaway. Even if he'd recorded the claim, that wouldn't deter most claim-jumpers who had little fear of getting caught in that remote region. Perhaps he should never have left until he'd taken his axe and hacked out all the gold ore Kismet could possibly carry. Then, no matter what happened, he'd have all he'd ever need, even if he had to put it in the bank or guard it night and day from robbers. He sighed and picked up his bedroll. The finding of gold was difficult; the keeping of gold was infinitely more challenging.

A fresh team was hitched and the passengers straggled back into the coach. Ten minutes later they were bouncing and swaying, eastbound, along the road. Mora squirmed, trying to think of something pleasant.

"Whoa!" The stage rolled to a stop in front of Sand Tank station and the driver set the foot brake. "Fifteen-minute stop to stretch!" he called down. "Supper stop at the next station."

The sun was well down the western slope

of a brassy sky, but had lost none of its vigor as Mora stepped stiffly down from the coach, holding the door for the others. Not surprisingly he was the only passenger debarking at this out-of-the-way stop. He unlaced the leather cover over the rear boot to retrieve his carbine.

He looked around for Quanto, but saw a white stranger unhitching the team.

Then Lila Strunk emerged and called to the driver who was wiping his face with his bandanna. "Zeke, there's some fresh coffee on the stove!"

"Whew! Thanks, Lila, but I think I'll pass. I'm already hot enough. I'll just take a dipper of your spring water."

As Lila turned to go back inside, she caught sight of Mora. Her face lit up. "Dan!" She sprang forward and threw her arms around his neck. He dropped his bedroll and rifle and hugged her close for several long seconds. Her hair retained a faint scent of wood smoke.

She pulled back to arm's length. "*You're* a welcome sight." Her eyes swept him up and down, taking in his new sand-colored pants, blue checked shirt, and leather vest. For comfort and practicality, he still wore the Apache moccasins. "You even smell of bay rum."

"I reckon it's some improvement over the last time you saw me."

"Come inside," she said, taking his arm. "You want some fresh lemonade? How about a little supper? It's nearly time, and I just fixed some bacon and flapjacks for myself. I didn't expect you back so soon."

He thought she was chattering on rapidly as if to keep him from climbing back into the stage.

"Slow down, Lila. I'm staying for a while. Where's Quanto?"

"Oh, he left for Yuma a few days back to work on the railroad."

"Is it that time already?" He felt foolish. "I've lost track of the date." Truthfully he wasn't even sure of the day of the week. "Who's the new hostler?"

"Jason Watley. The company furnished him to finish out here until we close down. I told 'em I had to have somebody reliable. He's OK. Keeps mostly to himself. Knows his work."

Mora nodded.

"I'll bring some lemonade out here in the shade and we can talk. We'll eat when the stage leaves."

Ten minutes later the driver was back on the box and slapping the reins over the animals. The coach lurched into motion and he swung the six-mule hitch out onto the Gila Road.

"I won't be seeing that sight much longer," Lila said wistfully, leaning her elbows on her knees. She turned and forced a smile at him, tiny crow's-feet fanning out from the corners of her eyes.

He thought the fine wrinkles gave her an impish look, rather than an aging one. He could picture what she must have looked like thirty years before. He got up from beside her on the bench under the giant cottonwoods and paced back and forth. He'd been sitting too long in that cramped stage.

"I'm glad you came back so soon," she said.

"Divine Providence."

"What do you mean?"

He picked up his bedroll from the ground, placed it on the bench, and began untying the cord lashing. "I came to repay the loan you gave me," he said.

"I told you I was in no hurry for that."

He made no reply as he fished out the rawhide sack. "Hold out both hands."

She cupped her hands in front of her, and he dumped a pile of the gold-laden quartz into them. The small nuggets and chunks of rich ore overflowed her hands, spilling into her lap.

"Oh . . . ! My God, Dan . . . ! What's all this?" The shock seemed to take her breath.

"That should repay the loan, with a little interest," he said casually, enjoying her discomfiture. "Of course, you'll have to convert it to dollars when you get to town."

"Repay the loan? Why, this is a fortune!" She lowered her voice and glanced furtively about. But the hostler was out of sight and sound near the stable. "Did you strike a gold mine?" She sounded incredulous.

"Yes," he said. "That's exactly what I did."

While she gathered the pieces of rich ore onto her apron and gazed at the glowing heap, he gave her a brief summary of his discovery.

"Finding lost treasure, just like we played at when we were kids!" she exclaimed, her eyes flashing. She no longer looked tired or worn down by the heat. "It's almost too good to be true. I suppose you registered the claim."

"I started to, but changed my mind."

"Why?"

"Any outlaw could just walk into the courthouse and locate the latest finds by looking at the public records. It's a claim-jumper's paradise."

"I see. You think you'd have to stay at the site and guard it all the time?"

"Or hire a tough armed guard," he said. "Claim-jumpers don't generally work alone. Without it being registered, I figure the remote location, the Apaches, the summer heat, and the fact that it's hidden in a cleft of the mountain will keep it safe for as long as I'll need it."

"Oh, the excitement and mystery of it! Wouldn't you love to know what happened to those two poor Franciscans you found murdered?"

"I sure would. From the looks of their sandals and robes, they've been there a very long time. If any early records of the missionaries exist, they're probably in the dusty archives of Mexico City or Spain."

She gathered the sagging apron close to her and stood up. "Well, let's go find a good place to hide this, and then have some supper. We can talk."

In spite of his earlier resolve, Mora felt drawn to this woman more than to any other he could remember. His shrewish, demanding wife had faded into his past — a past of pressure and worry and unjust accusations in a world he could hardly realize he'd ever inhabited. "Until I found it again, that mine had been safely hidden for at least a hundred years, and probably longer," he said, following her toward the cottonwood log station.

"You know I can't accept all this," she said over her shoulder. "This is ten times . . . no, a hundred times more than I lent you."

"We shook hands on the standard arrangement. Remember? You'd get half of any discoveries I made."

"I know, I know, but I never. . . ."

"Never expected me to strike it rich?"

"Frankly . . . no. It was a remote possibility, of course, but. . . ."

"Then be quiet and accept your good fortune."

"Dan, I can't. Maybe I'll take only a little more than I gave you, but not all this."

"Let's just say that interest rates have gone up. You're now a silent half partner in a mine."

"Daniel Mora, I don't know what I'm going to do with you."

"I can think of a thing or two."

He thought her face reddened under the deep tan as he held the plank door for her to enter.

"How long can you stay?" she asked.

"A day or so. Have to get the next stage back. Left my burro boarded at the livery in Castle Dome Landing. And I'm already getting paranoid about someone finding that mine. I've had to spend some of the flakes and nuggets on my traveling expenses, and that always arouses curiosity, especially from the wrong people. You never know who you can trust. By the way, I've named it the Saint Francis."

"Untie my apron," she said.

He pulled the bow loose behind her waist, and she carefully set the heavy load on the table, then turned to face him. The red glow of the setting sun shone through the glass-less window, making her skin look as bronze as an Indian's. Only her blue eyes and delicate features gave away her heritage. "So, what are your options?" she asked.

"As I see it, I can dig as much out of that vein as I can, then hide it somewhere else, put it in the bank, convert it to coin or greenbacks, invest it, or record the claim and sell it, or donate it to charity."

"Dan, my good friend, I wouldn't be in your moccasins for anything," she said. "Nearly every day I see men travel through on the stage, men who'd slit your throat . . . or mine . . . without batting an eye, for a tenth of what's lying on that table. Even if there wasn't any danger from killers and robbers, there're the Indians. And if that weren't enough, 'those to whom much is given, much will be required.' A Biblical quote, I believe."

"I know. Thought I'd left that old crushing sense of responsibility behind in California. But it's been weighing me down all the way from Castle Dome."

"Perhaps I can ease your burden while you're here." She slipped her arms around his neck and kissed him.

Chapter Fourteen

The warm morning breeze stirred gray-green leaves of a gnarled cottonwood that stood silently sucking moisture through its deep roots beside the shallow water of the Gila River.

A chaparral cock, commonly called a road-runner, strutted, stiff-legged, with tail feathers erect, along the sandy road near the base of the rough-barked tree. It paused and turned its red-eyed glare toward the trickling stream. With blurring speed, it snatched a tiny gecko, torpid from the warming rays of the early sun. Breakfast squirming in its pointed beak, the bird darted into a mesquite thicket and vanished.

High overhead, a hawk hung, motionless, on the rising thermals, keen eyesight probing the brush below for a stray rodent returning late to its burrow. The raptor ignored two dark figures that moved along the dun-colored desert. They walked upright like men, and came haltingly toward the river from the south. A half-dozen black vultures appeared to follow them, drifting like pieces of charred paper against the blue sky. The vultures soared effortlessly, patiently awaiting their inevitable meal; instinct and experience told them the two men who staggered and wobbled along would soon be carrion.

A half mile away, a mule-drawn wagon rattled eastward along the Gila Road, and the broad-winged hawk banked away to hunt prey farther from these disturbances.

The sun was well up, but Hugh Deraux kept pushing Angel Rivera ahead, instead of stopping to rest. The Mexican still carried the mule gut looped over his shoulder, but it was now limp, the nauseating water it contained nearly gone. Even with severe rationing, enforced by Deraux's Colt, they were down to less than a pint of glutinous liquid. It was now or never. After several nights of walking, they would have to push for the Gila River, or die. They could not last another night. Thus, they continued after sunup.

Deraux had lost track of the number of days and nights they'd struggled northward from the Tinajas Altas. He had only disjointed recollections of hours and hours of trudging across the moonlit desert, the Mexican in front, carrying the mule gut. Thank God for the roasted mule they'd eaten before they started. Without that, Deraux knew the kangaroo rat and the small lizard they'd managed to catch and eat raw would not have sustained them this far. The distasteful pulp of a small barrel cactus Deraux had gashed open with the Mexican's knife had done little to allay their all-consuming thirst and save their water. They'd crossed northwest between the Copper Mountains and the Cabezas Prietas, then a long stretch of desert before they finally struck the Mohawk range where they hoped to find more granite tanks of water.

But their hopes had been dashed. The two enemies had stood, side-by-side, staring at the shallow depressions they'd struggled so far to reach — depressions containing only a crusty, scaly residue where once there'd been rain water during the rainy season. But the rainy season had long passed. Deraux's raging thirst erupted anew with this disappointment, and he had trouble swallowing. The mucous membrane in his mouth and throat was drying up like glue. But he never winced, never let on to Rivera that he was

241

close to the point of despair, even when the Mexican whined and cursed, his dry throat roughing his voice like the croaking of some strange animal. When the Mexican snatched up the end of the mule gut and began sucking water from it, Deraux clubbed him across the head with the barrel of the Colt, splitting open his scalp. The Mexican cursed and howled, reaching for his head. But only a trickle of blood seeped out. His life-giving blood was drying up. Nevertheless, Deraux wouldn't allow the Mexican to guzzle their precious water. They had to make it last until they found another source. And the closest water was the Gila River, at least another thirty miles to the north.

Deraux squinted at the irregular line of vegetation ahead that signaled the course of the Gila. They'd made it, but he steeled himself against letting down too soon. They had to be sure the river was not bone dry, although various springs always kept some water in the Gila, even in the driest times. The Mexican shuffled along, head down, like a foundering horse; he'd not yet noticed the cottonwoods marking the watercourse 200 yards ahead.

Deraux inhaled deeply to gather his last strength as they approached the river. He heard the musical burbling of water over rocks and swayed forward, falling to his hands and knees by a clear pool of water. He thrust his face into it, sucking up the precious fluid, gulping it down, letting it wash over his cracked lips and crusty, whiskered chin. He vaguely heard Rivera's inarticulate cry as he threw his whole body into a shallow pool a few yards downstream. Until the Mexican recovered somewhat, Deraux knew he had nothing to fear from him, and continued to drink.

Deraux finally rocked back on his haunches and felt for the Colt in his belt as Rivera staggered to one side, then went to his knees, wretching.

"Too much, too fast," Deraux muttered, watching this display with no emotion. Then he heard a creaking, rattling of an approaching wagon, and stood up.

The driver pulled the span of mules to a stop twenty yards away. Two other men in the wagon had rifles across their arms.

Keeping one eye on the sick Mexican, Deraux walked toward the wagon. His knees seemed strangely stiff, as if his joints needed grease. He held up both hands, palms outward, in what he hoped was a friendly gesture. He was relieved to see these were white men, dressed in denim work clothes, and not Mexican bandits. Yet, white men or not, they could still be outlaws, although the lack of mounts said otherwise.

"How far to the next stage stop?" Deraux asked, his unused voice hoarse.

" 'Bout fifteen mile east," the driver replied after some hesitation.

"Which one would that be?"

"Sand Tank station."

"Shore could use a lift," Deraux said. "We're about done in." He kept his hat on, hoping his short hair would not give him away as an escaped convict. If these men were from Yuma, they'd probably heard about the break out.

"Where you boys been?" one of the men in the back of the wagon asked suspiciously, a carbine in the crook of his arm.

"Doing some prospecting. Got lost in the desert," Deraux lied, hoping he sounded convincing. He gestured at Rivera, sitting on the ground by the water. "Had to shoot our mule for food and use his gut to hold water from one o' those tanks in the mountains yonder."

"Not many men prospect in the desert this time o' year," the man with the carbine said.

Deraux snorted a harsh laugh. "You can bet we won't try it again. Thought we'd go in summer when it might be safer from Injuns." He didn't blame these workmen for being suspicious if he looked as disreputable as the Mexican — lean as a hungry wolf, sun-blistered skin peeking through holes in ragged shirt and pants, cut-off boots wrapped in rags to keep the soles on, several days' growth of ratty whiskers, crusted with dried sweat.

Deraux said nothing further and the three workmen sat silently regarding this apparition from the desert for a long minute before anyone spoke.

"I reckon we can give you a ride as far as we're going," the driver finally said.

"You're not going to Sand Tank station?"

"No, we'll be cutting off to the south up ahead about ten miles."

Deraux motioned to Rivera to come as he stepped toward the wagon, making sure to keep his hands away from the Colt in his belt. "What kind of work you men doing?" he asked, climbing up onto the wheel hub and into the back.

"Surveying for the Southern Pacific," one of them answered.

"Thought most o' that would have been done by now," Deraux said in an effort at conversation to put the men at ease. He noted the tripod and instruments in the wagon bed, along with bedrolls and camp gear.

Rivera wiped his mouth with a sleeve and wobbled toward the wagon.

"The grading crew will be following behind us in a couple of weeks," the driver said, clucking the mules into motion as the third man reached down to help the Mexican over the tailgate.

Deraux kept the conversation light and friendly, trying to divert suspicion, discussing the prospects of the stage companies after the railroad was built. The surveyors said little, and finally Deraux stopped talking. He was thirsty again, his body not having absorbed as much water as it needed. He sat propped against the sideboard of the wagon, keeping a wary eye on Rivera. The fight seemed to have gone out of the Mexican, but Deraux knew it would not pay to let down his guard. The man was as wily and dangerous as a sunning sidewinder.

The wagon bounced and rattled along for several miles over the rutted Gila Road, that trended toward the river, then away from it. Finally the driver pulled up. "This is where we turn off."

"Thanks, gents." Deraux climbed out and the Mexican slid off the tailgate.

"About another four or five miles down

that road will fetch Sand Tank station. Or, if you're tired of walking, there's an eastbound stage due along this evening."

"Thanks."

Deraux gave the stony-faced men a friendly wave as the wagon rolled away on a faint track toward the south.

They stood until the wagon grew small in the distance before they started walking east. Deraux was glad these surveyors were not going into any civilized areas where they could report the two men they'd picked up. The water and the ride in the wagon had renewed their strength. They stopped several more times to drink from the river. It seemed a strange luxury to have water anytime they took a fancy for it.

It was nearly noon when the cottonwood-log station came in sight. A wisp of smoke at the stone chimney indicated a cooking fire, and Deraux's stomach growled. The water had revived his system and stirred up his appetite.

"Give me back my knife," Rivera said as they neared the station.

"Hell, no."

"There's a woman runs this station. I want t'cut her gizzard out." The Mexican's eyes were narrow slits in his dark face.

"Why?"

"I worked here as a hostler. She fired me for some damned Indian."

"No reason you should kill her."

"No white woman treats me like that and lives."

"Never saw a damned greaser so full of pride it wasn't leakin' outta his ears."

Rivera turned such a look of pure hate in his direction that Deraux felt a chill pass over him in spite of the heat. He placed a hand on his Colt. "Cool off. Keep your mouth shut, and let me do the talking. You make a move to start something here, I'll kill you. Got that?"

Rivera said nothing.

"Is the Injun still the hostler?"

Rivera shrugged.

"How long since you been here?"

"Three weeks or so."

"What tribe's this Injun?"

"Tarahumara."

"As long as he weren't no Apache or Yuma or one o' the local tribes hereabouts."

The men headed toward the door.

"We'll get something to eat and then wait for the eastbound stage tonight," Deraux said. "I've still got that money we took offen those Mexican crap shooters in Yuma. I want to get as far away from the territorial prison as I can. And you're coming with me

248

until we get down to San Antone, where I can disappear without you trying to turn me in for the reward." With a glance toward the adobe stables and corral, Deraux opened the plank door and the two men entered the low-ceilinged room. The delicious aroma of frying steak assaulted his nose.

"Watley, wash up outside. It's about ready. You get that harness mended?" came a woman's voice from the kitchen-anteroom.

"It ain't Watley, ma'am," Deraux said.

Lila Strunk appeared in the doorway. Deraux saw the middle-aged woman's face blanch and her eyes grow wide as she stared at the dark, wolfish countenance of Rivera. "You! What're you doing back here?"

"Give us food and water," Rivera said.

She glanced at the open door behind them, as if looking for her hostler or the stagecoach that wasn't due for hours. "Where're your horses?"

"Just bring out that meat I smell," Rivera demanded, moving toward the table.

"Get the hell outta here!" she burst out.

"Ma'am, bring the food," Deraux said in a civil tone. "We ain't here to hurt you. Just give us some food and water and we'll be on our way east as soon as the stage comes in."

"You got any money?" she asked.

"None that you're getting!" Rivera said.

"We'll have to be in your debt," Deraux said a little more gently. It went against his nature to be cruel to women, unless he was riled.

"My hostler will be in shortly," she said.

"Get the grub out here now!" Rivera snapped.

"So you've decided to talk English. You never did that when you worked here."

"Why bother? With you looking down your nose at me like I was horseshit, I wasn't gonna make it any easier for you. You could just speak *my* language."

This woman had sized them up quickly, Deraux thought as the two of them slid onto the benches opposite each other at table. He'd noted her eyes taking in the Colt in his belt and glancing toward Rivera's boot top where he used to carry his knife.

A minute later she reappeared with a tray of sizzling steaks and potatoes, along with a bowl of beans.

Rivera tore off a hunk of the flatbread and began scooping up the beans, snatching at his food like a ravenous wolf.

Deraux reached across and removed the Mexican's sharp table knife before he got any ideas about using it. A footfall at the doorway made him look up.

"Oh, Jason, come in," Lila said, obviously relieved.

A wiry, muscular man, the hostler was wiping his hands on a towel, then began rolling down his sleeves as he regarded the two ragged men at table.

Deraux noted a warning glance pass from Lila to Jason Watley. The hostler was not wearing a gun. "You gents go right ahead," Watley said. "Lila and I will set outside and eat. We have business to talk over."

He and Lila collected two tin plates and filled them.

Feeling the tension in the room, Deraux got up and moved to the inside pump, tin pitcher in hand. Rivera was still stuffing his mouth as fast as he could chew and swallow.

On a sudden impulse, Deraux pulled his Colt. "You folks sit right down over there where I can keep an eye on you," he said. He hated tipping his hand so early, but he couldn't take a chance on letting this pair out of sight. Watley or the woman probably had a shotgun or rifle stashed close by, and he couldn't afford to let them get their hands on it.

Rivera looked up, his mouth full.

Lila Strunk and Jason Watley moved

across the room and sat down on a bench next to the wall, holding their plates on their laps.

"Not that I don't trust you," Deraux said, placing the Colt on the table as he picked up his fork, "but I know you think we're a couple of desert rats who are here to rob you. You'd be wrong. We don't mean you no harm. We're just about half starved and I want to keep everything quiet and peaceful until we leave."

An uncomfortable silence ensued while the four of them ate.

"You going to keep that gun on us until the stage arrives?" Lila asked, standing up and placing her plate and fork in a bucket of water. "What then?"

Deraux was already anticipating that problem. He might have to change his plans about catching the eastbound stage. He said nothing as he finished off his meal with another drink of water. He and the Mexican had been up all the previous night, struggling across the desert toward the Gila. Lack of sleep and now the food combined to drag him down. He couldn't stay alert much longer to guard these two. But he was even more wary of Rivera. The minute he dozed off, the Mexican would seize a knife to slit his throat, or shoot him with his own gun.

"We might have to borrow a couple of your animals and ride on outta here," Deraux said, formulating a plan as he spoke. "We'll leave them at the next station." He picked up the Colt and came around the table to stand in the middle of the room. "In fact, I think a better idea would be to leave Rivera here, so you two can get re-acquainted." He grinned.

"You leave me here with that bitch, I'll kill her!" Rivera said.

"Not if I leave your dead body."

"You may be a damned convict, but you ain't no killer."

He was right. Deraux knew he could bring himself to kill only in self-defense. He'd been convicted of stage robbery, but he didn't want to add murder to his record. He must decide quickly.

"Get up from there and search this place," he ordered Rivera. "Take any food or money you can find and throw it in a sack. Then we'll take two of the stage horses and light out."

Rivera grinned at being given license to ransack his former boss's orderly station, and went at it with a will while Lila and her hostler stood helplessly by.

253

Holding the Colt, Deraux moved to where he could watch the Mexican go into Lila's adjacent living quarters, a tiny room off the main station. Rivera kicked open the wardrobe, threw her clothes on the floor, smashed the pitcher and bowl on the bedside table. He yanked the pillow and thin mattress off the bed and a pistol clattered to the floor.

"Pick that up, easy like, and slide it over here," Deraux said.

When the Mexican complied, Deraux shoved the long-barreled Colt under his belt, still holding the other weapon.

A cedar chest was locked, but Rivera took out his fury on it with his boot. The wood finally splintered and the lock sprang open. He rummaged inside.

"By God!" He rooted down farther, slinging clothes aside. "Look at this!" He swiveled on his haunches, holding up a chunk of white quartz. Even from several feet away, its gold content was obvious to Deraux. He was stunned.

"There's more of it!" Rivera could hardly contain himself as he brought out a double handful of the ore and dropped it on the floor. "She's rich." He plunged in up to his shoulders once more. "That's all of it," he said, several seconds later. The softly glow-

254

ing pile caught the sunlight on the rough planks.

"Where'd you get it?" Deraux asked.

"My husband and I saved it up over the years."

"That's a damned lie. Nobody gets paid with gold ore like that. That rock is from the mountains somewhere. Maybe not too far from here," Deraux said.

For once, Rivera seemed speechless, fondling the gold, and spreading it out around him on the floor.

"Where'd you get it?"

She was silent.

Jason Watley looked from the gold to Lila and back with an astonished expression.

"It's best that you tell us," Deraux said, already thinking to set himself up for life, far from this place and the clutches of the law.

"There's plenty there. Take it and leave," she said.

"You tell us where you got it and we will."

She set her jaw grimly.

"Everyone back into the dining room," Deraux said, gesturing with the pistol.

As they moved toward the table in the center of the room, Deraux went to the open door and glanced out. The desert road was empty in both directions.

"All right, lady, I've asked you nicely. Either tell us where that gold ore came from, or I'll have to turn Rivera loose on you."

The Mexican gave a wolfish grin.

Watley glared his hate at Deraux.

"A business associate of mine left that here. He'll be back for it later, and pay me for looking after it," she said, her voice trembling. "Said he was afraid to have Wells Fargo ship it east because of all the stage robberies."

"Where'd he get it?"

"I don't know. He wouldn't tell me. Said it would be better if I didn't know."

"What's this man's name and where did he go?"

"I can't tell you that. Just take the gold and go."

"When Rivera gets through with you, you'll be begging to tell me everything you know." Deraux was bluffing, but she didn't know it. He thumbed back the hammer on his Colt, then drew Rivera's knife from his belt and tossed it to the Mexican. "Use this on her until she talks. And if you have any ideas of throwing that at me, you'll be a dead man before it leaves your hand."

An hour later, Deraux had the knife back.

He and Rivera, gold and food in their saddlebags, canvas bags of water slung across their pommels, were riding two of the stagecoach mules west. To keep from meeting anyone, they stayed north of the Gila Road, riding parallel to the river, through as much thick mesquite as they could find.

Deraux was satisfied with a good day's work. He'd let Rivera scare the woman, more than hurt her, although she wound up with several burns, cuts on her throat, and the threat of death ringing in her ears. She and the hostler, Jason Watley, had been left secured with harness straps and rope inside two of the stable stalls. They would be found and released by the driver and guard of the next stage, and no harm done. But she'd revealed that the gold had come from a man named Daniel Mora who'd found the vein, she said, in the Castle Dome region and was on his way there now to continue digging the rich ore out of his unrecorded mine.

Deraux was inclined to believe her story, since she feared for her life when she blurted out this information. And Rivera knew this Daniel Mora on sight. It was his Indian, Quanto, who'd been given Rivera's job as hostler. This made the Mexican seem all the more eager not only to find Mora and take his gold, but also to take his life.

CHAPTER FIFTEEN

Lyle Coopersmith stepped out of the adobe stable and watched the stage driver and three passengers help Lila Strunk toward the log station. He'd quickly seen that she wasn't badly hurt, so had stood back and let the others soothe and console her. But from what he'd observed of Lila Strunk, she was not a wilting flower who needed much fussing over.

Jason Watley came up alongside, flexing his arms and rubbing the red marks on his wrists where the harness straps had bound them for several hours. "That damn' Mex would 'a' cut me, too, if he thought I could 'a' told 'em anything," the hostler said.

"Are you injured?" the Englishman asked as the two of them started toward the station.

"Naw. Just stiff and sore. Out here, a man expects that kinda treatment from the Apaches, but not from a white man or a Mex."

"Mister Watley, you and Missus Strunk are very fortunate those two were *not* Apache Indians, or we would not be having this conversation," Coopersmith said. He paused and took off his hat to mop his face with a large red bandanna. Except for under the sweatband, his face was hardly damp; he felt only the grainy salt of dried perspiration. Yet he preferred this desert heat to the moist tropics of several of Her Majesty's colonies. The blazing orb that had pressed down on them all day was at last resting on the horizon, casting long shadows of men, horses, bushes, and buildings. The sky was cloudless, lacking even the usual spectacular gold and red sunset Coopersmith had come to expect. He looked forward every evening to the panoply of colors that was a partial compensation for the daily heat.

"Where did these men come from and what were they after?"

"Mister Coopersmith, I. . . ."

"Coop will do."

"Coop, I don't have the foggiest notion. They just appeared out of the desert on foot. I didn't even see 'em till I went in to lunch, and then the white man pulled a gun on me and Lila."

"Robbery, I presume. But what would

anyone expect this place to have that's worth taking?" the Englishman mused aloud to himself. "Perhaps the stock?"

"Those two half-starved scarecrows could 'a' scared off a buzzard. They was burned-out, dirty, ragged, and looked mighty near done in. A couple o' desert rats on their last legs if I ever seen 'em. They was out to grab whatever they could get their hooks on."

"What did they take besides a couple of mules and saddles?"

"I . . . think I'll let Lila answer that, if she's of a mind."

Coopersmith looked his curiosity at Watley as they entered the dining room of the station. Lila was stretched out on the floor on a mattress someone had dragged in from her bedroom. A young woman passenger was using a wet cloth to clean off the superficial cuts on the stationkeeper's neck. Two male passengers, the guard, and the driver were all crowded around her.

"Ah, Mister Coopersmith." Lila smiled, catching sight of him. She started to rise, but the woman restrained her.

"You better take it easy, missus," the woman said.

"I been taking it easy all afternoon in that stable," she said irritably. "I'm all right." She shoved the woman's hand away. "Just a few scratches. Thanks for your help." She pushed herself erect. "I'm really dry. Hand me that dipper."

The guard scooped a gourd full of water from the bucket under the pump and passed it to her. She gulped it down and handed it back. "Again."

After a second drink she seemed to catch her breath, and Coopersmith noted some color returning to her face.

"Lila, I think you and Watley need to gather up your things and come with me," the lanky, mustachioed driver told her solicitously. "We'll trail the extra horses behind the stage to the next home station. This place has gotten too dangerous. The company will be shuttin' 'er down afore long anyhow. It ain't worth anybody's life to stay here. Apaches got your husband a few months ago, and now this. . . ."

"Charley, I'm staying!" Her tone cut off further argument. She turned to her hostler. "Watley, help get a fresh team harnessed. These folks need to be on their way. Sorry there ain't any supper, folks," she announced, "but the robbers took most o' the grub, too."

The driver gave a tight grin as she began to sling orders. "Yes, *ma'am*."

Ignoring the fresh cuts still oozing blood

262

and serum down onto the collar of her dress, she took Coopersmith by the arm. "Let's go outside. I need to talk with you."

"You feel up to it right now?" Coopersmith asked when they moved toward the huge cottonwood near the spring.

"I'm all right," she said impatiently. "Just hurt my pride that I let that slippery Mexican get the best o' me. I was off my guard since I never expected him to show up here again."

"Did you know the man with him?"

"Never laid eyes on him."

"Describe him."

"Tough-looking character. Maybe forty years old. About five ten, lean and hard, prominent nose, dark hair, hadn't shaved in a couple weeks, but his whiskers were about as short as the hair on his head."

"Bald?"

"No. When he took off his hat, it looked like his hair was just growing out from having his head shaved. Seemed to have a little more class than Rivera. Talked nicer to me. Even took off his hat when he came inside, automatic like, as if it were a habit. Maybe had decent parents who taught him manners a long time ago."

"Or prison guards who'd beat it into him . . . ," Coopersmith murmured.

"What?"

"Several convicts broke out of the territorial prison while I was in Yuma," he said. "Four or five got away. This man could be one of them. The prisoners have their hair cropped close to their skulls."

"Come to think of it, Rivera did refer to him as a damned convict." She looked toward the others who were milling about and conversing some thirty yards away. Three of the men worked at unhitching the team. "I want to talk to you about something else," she said, touching his sleeve. "Word will get out about this before long, anyway," she began. "Did Watley tell you what they stole?"

"Food, mules. Said you'd have to tell me the rest."

"They took a sack of very rich gold ore."

Coopersmith was stunned into silence. Apparently his face conveyed his surprise.

"That's right," she said. "Gold ore. Daniel Mora gave it to me last week when he came back to repay the grubstake I'd given him. Probably worth several thousand dollars. Much more than the grubstake. He told me he'd struck a mine that'd been hidden in the mountains for more than a hundred years."

"Do you think those desert rats somehow

knew the gold ore was here?"

She shook her head slowly. "No. I believe it was just an unlucky break for me. When Rivera pulled it out of my cedar chest, he looked as shocked as you did just now. I don't have a safe to keep valuables, and he just stumbled upon it when he was ransacking the place."

Coopersmith rubbed a hand across his dusty mustache and stared toward the afterglow in the western sky.

"But that's not the worst of it," she continued. "That Mex tortured me with burning sticks from the stove and with a knife until I told them where I got it. I tried to lie, but they sensed it and began to slice me even worse. Rivera threatened to slash my throat and leave me dead . . . and Watley, too. I'm terrified of knives, so I wound up telling the truth. Now I'm sure they've ridden off to find Mora and take his mine, and maybe kill him. Rivera hates Mora because he persuaded me to fire Rivera and hire the Indian, Quanto, in his place for pay."

"I'm not trying to find out where this mine is, but did Mora tell you anything at all about the location of it?"

"Mister Coopersmith, I've always been a good judge of character, and I trust you, or I wouldn't be telling you any of this. Daniel said his discovery was in the Castle Dome mining district."

"That's a good-size area of mountainous desert north and east of Yuma. If this hard-case with Rivera *is* an escaped prisoner, he's taking a big chance riding back toward the territorial prison."

"Some men will risk anything for gold, even life itself."

"If it's any consolation, I'm not one of those men."

"Mind you, I was hog-tied in the stable and didn't actually see them leave, but the hoof beats sounded as if they were heading west."

"Makes sense, if they took that much trouble to get the information out of you."

"Daniel also told me he'd decided not to record the claim."

"Why?"

"Because that would make its location a matter of public record, and he couldn't physically defend his discovery all the time. He thought secrecy was the best strategy."

Coopersmith nodded. "That's one more obstacle in the way of those two finding Mora's mine."

"Where are you going from here?"

"Back to the construction gang that's working east from Yuma. I gave myself a short holiday to travel this far for a visit, and to work up my notes. I'm debating hiring a photographer to record some images of railroad construction for my book, but that may be too expensive."

"I . . . have a favor to ask," she said hesitantly, dabbing with a bandanna at the cuts on her neck.

"Name it."

She was silent for a moment. "As long as you're returning west, could you try to find Daniel Mora and warn him of the danger?"

"He's a good man, sure enough," Coopersmith stalled, unsure of what his answer would be. He knew Lila considered Mora more than just a friend in trouble. But Coopersmith had long since learned to stay clear of other people's personal attachments. "You can bet I will," he finally said. "I'll start this very night, but will require a horse from you."

"You don't have to leave right away. Morning will be soon enough."

"I'd prefer to travel at night when it's cooler. I can make better time and there's less danger from Apaches and of losing my way, as long as I stick to the Gila Road."

"I really hate asking you to do this," she said as they walked back toward the stagecoach. Watley and the driver and guard were just backing a fresh team into place and hooking them up.

"To tell you the truth, I was getting bloody bored with watching men build a railroad. There are only so many questions one can ask and only so many interviews one can conduct with the foremen and the workers who speak English. I'm ready for a little excitement, and this might just provide it. The only thing is . . . finding Mora in that maze of desert mountains will be difficult, especially if he's nervous and watching his back trail, not wanting to be seen. I don't consider myself an intrepid outdoorsman and tracker." He smiled at her. "But I'll certainly have a go at it."

"If it's any help, he did say he'd left his burro at the livery in the little Colorado River town of Castle Dome Landing. Might give you a place to start."

Coopersmith didn't admit it aloud, but he'd acquiesced to her plea only because he planned to revisit the Southern Pacific grading crew and somehow persuade Quanto to leave his job and join him. He realized he *must* have the help of a skilled tracker; he couldn't depend on his own blind luck to locate Mora in those mountains.

"As long as you insist on remaining, I'll stay

for a few days as well and help you." The sole woman passenger, Anna Withers, was firm in her resolve. She was about thirty, full-bosomed, with upswept dark hair. "No objections!" She held up her hand as Lila started to say something. "I'm an Army wife and have nothing better to do at the moment. I was on my way from Fort Yuma to meet my husband at Fort McDowell, near Tucson. I've given the driver a note to let my husband know what happened to me. I'll take a later stage." She reached to drag her oval grip from the rear boot as the other passengers were climbing back into the stage.

"Watley can take care of things until I'm feeling better," Lila objected.

The younger woman arched her dark eyebrows. "Just like he was a great help this time?"

Lila said nothing.

"Do you have any guns here?" Anna asked.

"The robbers took my Colt, but there's a double barrel shotgun in the stable one of the stage messengers left for the hostler, and I've got a case of shells for it."

"Good. We'll bring it in here and make sure it's in working order. I travel with a Thirty-Eight Colt Lightning in my duffel, and I know how to use it. But, for now, I want to get some disinfectant and clean bandages on those neck wounds, then we'll scare up something to eat."

Lila looked grateful, but also seemed eager to deflect this smothering attitude by turning to Coopersmith. "Get some food before you leave. There're tortillas and a pot of cold beans."

"I'll manage. Don't worry about a thing."

"Then let me show you where my saddle horse is. Rivera and his *amigo* took two of my best mules. Guess they preferred animals they thought were a little hardier for desert travel." She guided him toward the stable, saying under her breath: "I know that woman means well, but I can do for myself here. I just got careless and let my guard down. A few days of her bossy attitude and I might be all for catching the stage out of here."

Coopersmith chuckled, and returned the wave of the driver as the stage swung out onto the Gila Road and turned east. Dusk was blanketing the isolated station.

"Watley, fetch out Pistol."

The hostler led up a gelding as Lila lighted the coal-oil lamp hanging on a nearby post. "He's not big, but he's durable," she assured him as Watley adjusted the Mexican saddle blanket over the animal's back. "He's got a lot of Arabian in him, a cross from one of Keene Richard's Kentucky purebred colts, I'm told. I've trained him to be ground-reined," she added. "He'll respond to any gentle, firm command, and he can run like the wind. He's been kept up too long and needs exercise."

"Perfect," Coopersmith replied. "If some of his ancestors are from the deserts of the Middle East, I'm certain he'll do fine."

Watley handed him an old, well-used California stock saddle. It was reasonably light he noted as he swung it into place. The saddle had a slim horn, deep seat with high pommel and cantle, and even pointed Spanish *tapaderas* hung from the covered wooden stirrups.

Ten minutes later, Coopersmith had tied on his bedroll, hung a full, blanket-covered two-quart canteen from the horn along with a cotton sugar sack of bread and dried goat meat. He gathered the reins and mounted.

"That bloodthirsty Rivera and his *compadre* have a seven hour head start on you. They looked pretty whipped out, so they'll likely camp somewhere along the trail. Be careful you don't ride up on them un-awares," Lila cautioned him, looking up in the yellow lantern light that illuminated the stable. Except for the inflamed, swollen burn on her lower lip, she looked as healthy as could be expected after her ordeal. A bandanna served as a temporary bandage around her lacerated neck.

"Rest assured, I'll be cautious," Coopersmith said, patting the holstered Colt he wore at his hip.

"Oh, and one more thing . . . ," Lila added. "Those two are traveling together, but they're *not* friends. In fact, Rivera appeared to be the other fella's prisoner."

"Odd. But then, there's no honor among thieves. They often fall out with one another. Now they have your gold to fight over as well. With any luck, their relationship will turn violent before long. Too bad there's no telegraph, or we could send a warning ahead to the law in Yuma."

She nodded. "The wire will follow the railroad, but not in time to help us. At least the stage driver, who just left, promised to report this robbery to the U.S. marshal at Tucson."

The territory is too vast and wild for that to do much good, Coopersmith thought. *I'm on my own.*

She laid a hand on the horse's nose and looked earnestly at Coopersmith. "You *must* find Daniel before they do." Her voice nearly broke, and she turned away.

Uneasy with this show of emotion, he simply said: "Keep your chin up. I'll see you soon."

He reined the horse around and rode off into the pre-moon darkness.

CHAPTER SIXTEEN

For the first hour, Lyle Coopersmith busied himself becoming accustomed to riding a Western saddle on an unfamiliar horse in the dark. Except for the stars, there was no light at all and he got far off the road twice before he realized that Pistol had a better instinct for finding his own way, so he let the gelding have his head. He was well trained, as Lila had indicated.

From having traveled it twice before, he was aware the Gila Road was not a road in the ordinary sense. It was merely a sandy wagon track that meandered back and forth roughly parallel to the Gila River. Its path varied according to weather, ruts, deep sand, and arroyos, winding wherever riders and stagecoach drivers decided to go, but rarely straying more than a mile from the river.

By the time he became comfortable with the horse and his direction of travel, a gibbous moon rose partially to light his way. It helped to some degree, but etched black shadows around every saguaro, mesquite bush, and cottonwood. As the night stretched longer, his fatigued mind imagined movements and potential ambush in every dark shadow.

When he stopped to let Pistol drink at the river, he decided he'd pushed himself far enough and sought a place to camp. 200 yards from the Gila, he found a large open area screened by mesquite on all sides. He unsaddled Pistol and hobbled him, then, not risking a fire, gnawed off a few bits of beef jerky and bread and washed it down with canteen water. He unrolled his blankets and stretched out, keeping his holstered Colt near at hand. Being unused to camping alone in the wild, his nerves at first kept him alert, sensitive to every strange noise.

Finally, when the moon began to wane, he dozed off and slept until early dawn. Then he rose, a bit stiff but feeling rested, quickly rolled up his bedding, and saddled the horse. Dawn reddened the eastern horizon as he put Pistol into an easy canter and the horse held the pace without tiring.

An hour later, with the sun well clear of the horizon, he watered the animal at the river and filled his canteen from a clear pool. Remounting, he headed southwest again. There was no sign of the two robbers, but he was careful not to ride through any thickets of brush or near any cottonwoods large enough to conceal a man.

By late morning the fierce sun had made travel unbearable. He sought relief, sheltering in the shade of desert scrub. The light, westerly breeze felt as if it were coming from a blast furnace. He unsaddled Pistol and let him roll in the loose sand to discourage the flies that quickly found him. Then he tied the horse to a large mesquite, and stretched out on the sand to doze and sweat through the hottest hours of the day.

The sun lay on the horizon when he roused himself from a heat-induced stupor and dashed a handful of canteen water into his face. He'd positioned the saddle blanket and was preparing to swing the saddle into place when he stiffened at the sound of hoof beats. Dropping the saddle, he caught hold of the bridle and placed his other hand over the horse's nose. Two mules came into view through the sparse vegetation. His heart began to race — the two riders fit the description of the robbers. The white man wore a tattered long underwear top and rode slightly behind the Mexican. The two were hard to tell apart, since both were burned dark from the sun.

Coopersmith held his breath as they came abreast of him. He heard the indistinct sound of a voice, followed by a sharp retort from the other. He prayed his horse would not move until the riders had passed. The horse seemed to sense the danger. But, at a critical moment, when the riders were within thirty yards of him, the muscles in Pistol's flank quivered and he swished his tail at the biting flies.

If the men hadn't been cursing each other, one of them might have noticed the movement through the scant brush. But the two rode on down the road, bouncing in the saddles to the mules' jarring trot.

Coopersmith let out a long sigh. Evidently he'd passed their camp in the dark.

In order to stretch out the distance between himself and this pair, he hobbled Pistol, then lay down for a half hour and reflected on the close call. Should he have confronted them, or attempted an ambush? That would have ended his need to find and warn Mora. But even with the element of surprise, he had neither the courage nor the skill to take on single-handedly two experienced and desperate gunmen. His part-Arabian Pistol wasn't even saddled, or Coopersmith might have tried to outrun them, had his ambush gone awry. They'd stolen Lila's Colt and were armed with at least two revolvers and a knife.

Satisfied he'd made the right choice, he consoled himself that he'd seen enough to recognize them later. He realized he was rationalizing. Truthfully it was fear that had paralyzed him into inaction. But a failed attack would have put them on their guard for later. Better they not know anyone was after them, except the law.

Perhaps he could overtake them tonight. But to have any chance, he'd have to creep close enough to shoot them in their sleep. And his conscience would call this murder. He closed his eyes. Too much thought, too little action. He definitely didn't have the instincts to be a lawman. The American Wild West he'd read about was just that — wild and lawless, a man's survival depending on his having few scruples. He wished he owned a rifle, since he was a much better shot with a long gun, and resolved to buy one when he reached Yuma.

A quarter hour later, he was at the river again, filling his canteen. As he bent over, he was startled at his reflection in the clear pool. The indistinct image staring back at him was that of a stranger. His sun-bleached hair needed a trim, his tawny mustache drooped over his mouth, and the flat planes of his face were as dark as they'd been in India. He grinned, his white teeth flashing in the dusky visage. "God Almighty, I look like a bloody, blond aborigine," he said aloud to his horse. At the sound of his voice, Pistol raised his dripping muzzle, then went back to drinking.

He capped his canteen and hooked it over his saddle horn. *Damn me, if I don't look fierce enough to scare hell out of anybody,* he thought. *But am I jelly inside?* He thought of his late father, Kensington Alton Cooper-smith — K.A. as he was known to his equals, and Professor Coopersmith to his many students. "Are you adequate to the task?" had been one of his father's favorite questions when probing, testing his pupils and his own children. Lyle paused, hand on the saddle horn, hearing his father's words as if the old man were standing beside him in the desert heat, high collar and cravat in place, waistcoat spotless, studying him through polished spectacles. Dead of apoplexy these twenty years, Kensington Coopersmith came out of the mists of time and death to challenge him. Lyle had a job to do. He must somehow find and warn Daniel Mora of the danger from the two robbers — that, or thwart them himself. Was he adequate to the task?

He took a deep breath and shook off the vivid image. *Yes, I am,* he thought, taking up the reins and swinging into the saddle. After throwing over a tame, low-paying clerical job to go adventuring in the colonies, he'd better be adequate to the task. He'd survived hair-raising scrapes halfway around the world, so there was no reason he couldn't keep his head about him and accomplish this job. Yet, reining westward, he tingled with the same nervous instinct he imagined a cat must feel when he'd reached his ninth life.

Coopersmith tugged his hat brim low to block the declining sun, and tried to put himself into the minds of these outlaws. They'd passed him in the heat of the day, apparently inured to the deadly, debilitating effects of the summer sun. They appeared to be worn down by some earlier ordeal in the desert and would likely make camp at dark and sleep the night away. Anxious as they might be to find Mora and his mine, these two hardcases probably had enough sense not to rush westward at a mule-killing pace, as long as they knew pursuit was not imminent. With a sack of rich gold ore in the saddlebags, and prospects of more, they would stay focused on their goal, and not provoke confrontation with other travelers. On the contrary, they'd lie low. Like shy rattlesnakes, they'd avoid contact, but would be deadly if surprised. Coopersmith resolved to avoid them. He knew they were on the Gila Road, but they didn't know he was.

At dark, he guided Pistol into a copse of small cottonwoods away from the river and made a dry camp. He quickly fell asleep, but was awake and on his way by the time the moon was silvering the landscape.

He rode at a steady pace and, when dawn lightened the sky behind him, caught sight of distant dark specks moving against the dun-colored desert. As he approached, the sun topped the horizon and these figures materialized into horses, oxen, and the gear of the Southern Pacific grading crew.

Coopersmith splashed across the shallow river to the north side where the men were just finishing breakfast and hitching the teams to the scrapers. He dismounted near the wagon of the foreman, Ellis MacLeod, and ground-reined Pistol.

"Well, Coop, I didn't look for you to be back so soon," the lean, muscular Scotsman greeted him. "Have some breakfast?"

"Sure." He took a fork and speared two cold flapjacks onto a tin plate, then drowned them in molasses from a pitcher. He sat, cross-legged, on the ground, away from the heat of the small cooking fire to eat, as MacLeod poured and handed him a cup of black coffee.

"Ambrosia for the gods," Coopersmith exuded a few minutes later, wiping up the remaining syrup with the last hunk of pancake and popping it into his mouth. He put his dish into a bucket of water and poured himself more coffee from the smoke-blackened pot that hung on a tripod over the fire.

MacLeod hunkered on the other side of the fire and regarded him over the rim of his tin cup. "You look a mite weary. Been traveling all night?"

"Most of it," Coopersmith admitted.

MacLeod said nothing, but was obviously awaiting some further explanation. Coopersmith had flagged the passing eastbound stage, expecting to be gone at least a fortnight, and now was back within three days, riding a strange horse.

"I can't stay. Is Quanto still on the job?" He cocked an eye at the workmen some fifty yards away.

"Sure is. One of the best damned workers I've got. Wish they were all like him . . . more work than gripes."

"I need to borrow him."

"Borrow?" MacLeod arched sun-bleached brows. "What for?"

"Need a red Indian I can trust, and he's the only one I know. Mora tells me he's a tracker and a fighter." He glanced around. "Do I have your word you'll keep this to yourself?"

The foreman nodded.

Coopersmith proceeded to relate the story.

"Sounds as if you need to get the Yuma sheriff in on this," MacLeod commented.

"I'll alert him, but I doubt he'll provide much help."

"Why's that?"

"Those two outlaws will likely avoid Yuma. A wanted poster probably already exists for one of them, if he's an escaped convict. I figure the sheriff and maybe one deputy have plenty to keep them busy right there in town without hiring a posse to go traipsing into the mountains looking for a couple of highwaymen from another part of the territory." He drained his coffee and set the cup on a rock. "I'm no outdoorsman. Mora told me this Indian can survive on little water, is good with a knife and gun, and isn't troubled by scruples, as are many whites. Best of all, like most aborigines who've lived close to the land, he has a sixth sense about danger and the natural world. I need him."

"He might not want to go with you. He won't be paid when he's off the job."

"If we can locate Mora, he'll give Quanto enough gold to make up for any lost wages . . . and then some."

MacLeod looked toward a group of men who were setting timbers to support a small trestle over an arroyo. Coopersmith picked out Quanto by the faded blue bandanna tied around his head. The other men, including the Chinese, wore hats. "There he is," the foreman said. "Go ask him. If he wants to go, I'll pay him off."

"I can't speak Spanish."

"He's picked up a good deal of English since he's been here," the boss said. "My orders and such. He doesn't have to rely on one of these Mexicans to translate like he did at first."

Coopersmith approached the Indian, who had just set down his end of a thick post. He was already sweating in the early morning heat. Coopersmith thought he was darker and more muscular than he remembered.

"Quanto, you know me . . . Coopersmith? Remember, I paid your stagecoach fare?"

The Indian nodded impassively, his dark

eyes steady.

Coopersmith motioned him away from the others, and explained in simple terms what he wanted. "You go with me to find Mora?"

"Mora, friend," Quanto said. "We find him, stop bad men."

"Ah, my eloquent native," Coopersmith muttered with relief. "Put about as succinctly as any man could. You ought to stand for Parliament." A great weight was lifted from Coopersmith. With a light-hearted confidence he hadn't felt in days, he motioned for Quanto to follow him. "Draw your pay. Then we'll go."

The foreman was already in his wagon, dragging out his metal cash box.

Finding a suitable mount proved more difficult. The laborers had ridden from end-of-track in wagons, and none of these horses or mules could be spared, even if there had been a saddle. Foreman MacLeod was the only one who had a saddle horse here, while all the draft animals were being used to draw scrapers and drag heavy timbers.

"Coop, this Indian can run with the best of them," MacLeod said, counting out the greenbacks and holding a ledger for the Indian to make his mark. "We're only sixteen miles from Yuma. He could jog alongside your horse and never be winded.

In fact, I think he'd rather travel by foot than horseback any day. You could pick up a buggy or another mount in town."

MacLeod conversed with Quanto in fluent Spanish, and the Indian nodded.

"Just like I figured," the foreman said, setting the cash box inside the tailgate. "He's been missing his running. He's ready to go."

Coopersmith felt foolish riding while the other loped alongside, but they followed the river and made frequent stops. He motioned for Quanto to take a turn on the horse, but the Indian waved him off.

"No. No."

By the time they reached the edge of Yuma, Quanto was showing signs of fatigue, more from the heat than just the exertion, it appeared. He was as perfect a physical specimen as any human Coopersmith had ever seen, including the tall Zulu tribesmen in South Africa who were also legendary long-distance runners.

It was noon, and blazing hot. Coopersmith sought a drink of water in a saloon for the two of them, but the Indian was not admitted. Coopersmith chose not to make an issue of it, and brought out a jug of water and tortillas wrapped around chopped meat and chile peppers.

Since Quanto was averse to riding horses,

Coopersmith guessed the Indian was probably a poor rider, anyway, so he rented from the livery a covered buggy, drawn by a single horse. Quanto stayed with the rented rig while Coopersmith shopped the mercantile for additional camp gear and cooking utensils. Since he was rapidly running short of money, he bought an old Henry .44, instead of the new Winchester '73 he wanted. The brass receiver would cast a bright reflection in the sun, but it couldn't be helped.

"You're lucky," the clerk said. "These are the last two boxes of Forty-Four rimfire cartridges I have in stock. Not a big demand for these any more. Most men have gone over to the Winchesters, Marlins, or Remingtons." He grinned. " 'Course the Army still sticks with their old single-shot Springfields."

"Yeah." Coopersmith was only half listening. His mind was already on their journey upriver to Castle Dome Landing. Lila had said that was the best place to start.

He'd seen nothing of the two robbers, nor did he expect they'd show themselves in town. If they needed anything from Yuma, they'd more likely steal or buy it at night. But, if the outlaws rode into the dry Castle Dome Mountains in August, they'd have to be equipped to survive.

The clerk loaded the flour sack with all the dry foodstuffs and pans and matches, canvas water bags, and other odds and ends. Coopersmith paid for them, pocketed his change, heaved the bag over his back, picked up the Henry, and stepped out into the sunshine.

Finding Mora would be difficult. But he felt his chances were a lot better with Quanto at his side. Maybe they'd get lucky.

CHAPTER SEVENTEEN

The paranoia Daniel Mora had experienced following his discovery of the gold had vanished. Sitting by his campfire in the long summer evening, he was at peace with himself and his situation. Gazing down the shallow valley, he reflected that it was normal to have felt shock and wonder, followed quickly by suspicion that everyone he saw was plotting to kill and rob him. Then had come the terrible weight of responsibility sudden riches represented. He had to remind himself that gold was simply a heavy, yellow metal. His other perceptions were only fantasies.

With the blade of his short axe, he heaped more coals around the lid of his small pot of beans and bacon, then lounged back on an elbow and breathed deeply of the clean, dry desert air. Before his discovery, he'd possessed everything he needed for personal happiness. Then, in an instant, his world had turned upside down, thrusting him from dirt-poor prospector to one of the wealthiest men in the territory. The good news had been as big a shock to his system as the news of some personal calamity might have been.

He was aware of the dangers his new found wealth presented; he just wasn't possessed by them. His harmonious balance had returned.

Several days earlier, when he'd retrieved Kismet from the livery at Castle Dome Landing, he'd also bought a stout mule named Billy.

A stop at the mercantile produced a wooden pack saddle, some heavy leather bags, and three coils of good hemp rope. This time, he wanted to haul out a much larger load of the rich ore. In a town founded as a supply depot for the strikes and developing mines in the district, the major topic of discussion was all things related to harvesting precious metals. Mora knew his purchases had not gone unnoted, but that fact didn't concern him.

Heading east from town, Mora rode the mule bareback and let Kismet carry the pack saddle loaded with the camp gear and water kegs. He made no attempt to hide their trail as they journeyed the few miles directly toward the area of his St. Francis Mine. He kept his loaded Marlin handy, along with his belted revolver. Riding on high ground whenever possible, he avoided narrow canons, and also took normal precautions when camping. But fear was no longer a factor; he'd wrestled down his own mental hobgoblins.

With the scarcity of water for the animals in the summer heat, he decided to make this a quick in and out trip. He'd even brought nosebags and enough grain to last Kismet and Billy about four days; three-fourths of it was already gone. Since he would require his animals to labor in the heat, hauling his heavy treasure, the least he could do was ensure they were in top condition for the ordeal.

In the morning he planned to go directly to his mine about a mile away, climb up into the cleft, and begin chipping off enough ore to fill the four leather drawstring bags. He'd have to lower the heavy bags by ropes from the ledge, then pack them on his mule, Billy, making sure the load was secure and balanced, then move away a couple of miles to camp for the night. It would be exhausting work in the heat, and he wondered if it would take him more than a day to fill the four bags. But it was a pleasant dilemma to contemplate as he reclined on his ground-cover a comfortable distance from the fire. Most men worked for wages as he'd once done, subject to all the bosses' human foibles — anger, revenge, greed, and political conniving. Now he'd eliminated the middlemen, and was picking his wages directly from Mother Earth.

The meal was ready and he carefully raked away the glowing coals, spooned out the steaming beans and bacon onto a tin plate, and lounged back to eat it with flat pan bread. A filling and satisfying meal, but he still had a hunger for potatoes. It was one of the few things he missed from his former life. *Must be something in my Irish heritage,* he thought and smiled to himself. Potatoes were just too bulky and perishable to carry. Dry beans, onions, bacon, smoked ham, jerky, cornmeal, and rice were easier to pack.

Out of the corner of his eye, he caught a flash of white. Two, then three forms moved against a distant hillside. He put down his plate and pulled his field glasses from their leather case. Mountain goats swam into focus as he adjusted the twin lenses. He watched the animals leaping nimbly from rock to rock up the steep, reddish-brown hillside, then finally disappear over the top.

A bit of childish doggerel surfaced from the mists of his memory:

If all the world were flat,
Where would the mountain goats be at?

Filled with contentment at the sight of the wildlife, he replaced the glasses in their case. Hawks, cactus wrens, small rodents, lizards, even the few poisonous reptiles seemed welcome company to him. Having lived among them for many months, he no longer felt alien. It was said that St. Francis of Assisi possessed such peaceful rapport with animals that wild creatures came to him without fear. Mora knew it was probably only a pious legend, but it gave him a closer spiritual kinship with his patron.

He glanced at Kismet and Billy, grazing on a few green leaves of the nearby mesquite bushes. It would be nice occasionally to have another person to talk to. But then, conversation often led to opinions, then to arguments and hard feelings and. . . . No — non-human creatures were fine company. One could not let down and be completely natural and open with humans. There was always an element of reserve, and a person had to be careful what he said and how he said it. Human communication was a real struggle — most of the time not worth the effort.

His meal finished, he scrubbed clean the metal plate, cup, and pot with white sand to conserve his water.

Kismet raised her head, curled her lip, and brayed loudly.

Mora dropped the frying pan and yanked his pistol from his belt, a chill going up his back. He pivoted, looking all around him.

The desert was as peaceful and quiet as before. Normally his burro brayed only at some unusual presence. Then he saw another mountain goat moving against the brown rock 100 yards away. He let out a long sigh and shoved the gun back under his belt. He only thought he was completely relaxed; his caution had merely gone underground.

The sun was lighting the tops of hills next morning when Mora paused below his mine. The pre-dawn breeze had ceased and the still air in the deep shadow of the narrow defile was already very warm. He didn't want to leave his mule and burro here, but once the sun was well up, the rock overhang above this dry wash provided the only shade within a mile. He let the animals drink their fill from one of the water kegs, then tethered them, by a long lead, to a jutting rock.

"The sooner started, the sooner done," he muttered to himself as he pulled off the pack saddle, water kegs, and camp gear and set them to one side. Then he spread a piece of netting on the ground and made a small pile of his full canteen, ore hammer, short-handled axe, Marlin carbine, Smith & Wesson revolver, cartridges, and four thick leather bags that would each hold approximately half a bushel. Drawing the net together at the top, he secured it to the end of a long coil of rope. Then, tying the loose end of the rope to his belt, he pulled on his leather gloves and began climbing the opposite wall of the defile.

The morning was still relatively cool, but, by the time he reached the ledge some thirty feet up, he was perspiring heavily. He paused to catch his breath, wondering if he was sweating because of the exertion or the excitement of having the wealth of the world at his fingertips.

He hauled up the net with his tools and weapons. He shoved the bundle ahead of him through the narrow aperture in the tilted rock, then crawled in after it. It was still nearly dark inside, and he'd forgotten to bring anything to make a torch. But the sun's rays would soon filter through the overhead cracks, so seeing would not be a problem during the long day.

He opened the netting and coiled the rope to one side. Then he loaded both his carbine and his pistol before uncorking the two-quart canteen and swigging a long drink. Impatient as he was to get to work, there was not yet enough light, so he sat down and waited.

Only then did he remember that he was sharing the cave with the two dead Franciscans. When the rising sun finally provided enough visibility, he dragged the brown-robed, mummified skeletons by the cowls over the stone floor and laid them head to foot along the wall where the huge slab of tilted rock formed a narrow angle. He hardly had to touch the partially disarticulated bones and parchment-like tissue, but the remains still made his flesh crawl. He stood for a moment, gazing at the desiccated corpses, wondering again who they were and what their story had been. Perhaps at this moment they were looking down on him, approving of his finding the gold for which they no longer had any use.

His claim marker still contained the slip of paper he'd left. So, apparently, no one had been here. When the light was finally bright enough, he pulled aside the dry mesquite bush and began chipping away with his rock hammer. At least the dead air in the cave was somewhat cooler due to the shade and the moisture seeping down one wall.

Time ceased for him as he worked. He became totally absorbed, hacking away at the white quartz with its imbedded gold. Now and then he paused to scoop the loose pile of ore into one of his leather sacks. To save weight, he'd later chip off as much of the rock as he could, retaining only the pure gold. Yet, most of the yellow metal was so enmeshed with the quartz that the ore would require smelting to separate.

Deeper into the vein, the ore became hard to reach. He swung the backside of his axe at the edges of surrounding rock, knocking off large chunks to give himself access to the twenty-inch wide vein that angled downward into the solid rock. At some remote point in geologic time, gases from the bowels of the earth had evidently forced up the molten metal, where it cooled and hardened in this fissure as nearly pure gold. It was up to him to extract as much as he could with hand tools. When the face of the vein was too far down to reach, he'd have to use dynamite.

The sun's narrow shaft of light began

lancing through the overhead crack, illuminating drifting dust that stuck to his sweaty skin. Turning aside to breathe cleaner air, he moistened his bandanna in the seepage on the moss-covered wall and wiped his face and neck.

There were only two problems with using dynamite. First, he had no experience handling explosives and could very well blow himself into small pieces. Second, a charge might bury the golden hoard just as easily as revealing more of it. The huge slabs of rock that were tilted together to form this cleft would not stand for any heavy blasting without caving in. He glanced at his take so far — two sacks filled with as much as he could lift. Two more to go. He analyzed his feelings. Gold fever in the form of unreasonable greed was not part of his make-up. But he was practical. It was harvest time and he had to make gold while the sun shone.

One other possibility suggested itself. He could use a singlejack, like hard-rock miners used before the invention of the steam-powered compressed air drill. A singlejack was really just a chisel and hammer, probably not long enough to chip out much of this ore. And a doublejack would require one man to hold a longer chisel while a second man swung the hammer. This procedure was not used actually to dig out ore. It was a laborious way of punching narrow holes in which to set blasting powder or dynamite. He'd have to go to Castle Dome Landing to obtain these tools. But that could wait, he decided, returning to work on the rock. He needed the help of a partner he could trust. He slammed the rock with the back of the single-bitted axe. Chips and dust flew as more of the rock shattered onto the floor. The only person who came to mind as a possible partner was Lila Strunk, and she might not be up to all this physical labor and dirt. Who else? Quanto — an Indian who couldn't speak English, but who'd proven himself a true friend and benefactor.

Blam! Blam! Blam! The hammer blows in the confined chamber made his ears ring.

He raked away the broken rock with his foot, then got down on his knees and reached into the declivity, hacking off more of the rotten quartz with his small ore hammer. The vein showed no signs of pinching out as it sloped slightly downward. No telling how much gold this bonanza contained. For now, he'd take out all the gold he could possibly reach.

Suddenly Kismet brayed loudly. Then again.

Startled, Mora rocked back on his heels and stood up, listening intently. He grabbed his Marlin that was leaning against the wall. He'd been so absorbed in his work that he'd forgotten to check outside now and then. He crawled through the opening, sliding cautiously to the edge of the outside ledge, and peered over. Two men were in the narrow cañon below, attempting to saddle his mule and burro. They were dressed like white men, although what he could see of their skin was darker than any Indian's.

He worked the lever of the Marlin and fired a warning shot. The slug splattered chips ten feet from the men. They jumped behind the skittish animals for protection, peering up at him. One of the men yanked a revolver and fired a wild shot in his direction. The bullet whined off rock over his head.

"Get away from those animals!" Mora yelled, lying flat on his belly on the hot ledge.

His answer was an oily laugh that made his skin crawl. "Ah, Daniel Mora, we meet again."

"Who the hell are you?" Mora yelled, keeping his head down. The voice had a slight Spanish accent.

"Your old friend, Angel Rivera, come to pay you a call."

"Who?"

"Don't tell me you have forgotten so soon?" the voice replied in a tone of mock injury. "You got me fired at Sand Tank station."

Mora felt a sinking sensation in the pit of his stomach. "Make tracks outta here, or I'll put a bullet in you!" He was in no mood to fool with this man.

Suddenly the other man spoke with a calm, authoritative voice. "It's too hot to stand here, hashing over old times," he said. "So let's get down to business. We heard you digging up there, so this must be where your gold mine is."

Mora was stunned. How had word leaked out?

"So we're going to take your animals and your water and move off a ways and wait for you to get real thirsty. We figure it won't be long before you're willing to trade all that gold you've dug out for a good drink from one of these kegs."

Mora's mind was in a whirl, trying to figure a way out of this situation. He didn't reply, but jacked another round into the chamber of his weapon. The racheting noise was loud in the midday stillness.

"I wouldn't be shooting down here if I were you," the voice said, "unless you want to hit your mule and burro."

"But then I could kill you, too, before you could get out of range. There's no other cover down there."

"I'm betting you won't shoot your own animals," the man countered. "But, if you try, I've got these kegs ready to dump over. You'll have a mighty dry time walking out of here. And you sure won't be packing any gold on your back." He paused. "Is the gold really worth your life?"

Mora wondered if this pair had arrived afoot. They likely had mounts somewhere out of sight, and water, too, or they wouldn't be so ready to destroy his. He silently cursed his luck. Everything had been going too smoothly. They obviously knew he had gold; there was no use wasting time denying it.

"If I give up my weapons, and the gold, will you let me ride out of here with my animals and the water?" he called without exposing more than one eye over the lip of the ledge. The heated rock burned through his thin shirt and cotton pants. He slid a hand under his belly and extracted from his belt the loaded pistol he'd been lying on.

"You can have your animals and the water

to ride out," the voice replied.

"You obviously know who I am," Mora said, stalling. "Who are you? I'd like to put a name to the low-down scum I deal with."

"The name's Hugh Deraux. You'll think scum before we're done with you, unless you do as I say."

"Anybody who runs with Rivera is scum," Mora replied, trying desperately to plan his next move.

"All this talk is making me thirsty," Deraux said. "What about you?"

"Let's quit fooling around. Let me kill him!" Rivera broke in.

"Come ahead and try!" Mora shouted. "I'd love a chance at you. It's not much of a climb up here. You can do it," he mocked.

Muffled cursing in Spanish came from below, followed by an explosive pistol shot. The bullet whanged off the ledge a foot from Mora's head. He inched backward.

"OK, what'll it be?" Deraux yelled. "Haven't got all day. You have one minute to decide."

Mora took a deep breath of the heated air. He'd left his hat inside and the fierce sun was boring into his throbbing skull. "I believe I'll just sit up here in the shade for now, with plenty of water and food, until my partner shows up this evening."

"You're a damned liar. You ain't got a partner. But, if that's the way you want it. . . ."

Mora heard a scuffing and carefully moved to one side and slid forward to peer over the edge. The two men were completely concealed behind the animals, busily roping together the four water kegs, and looping a line from the loaded pack saddle to the mule's neck. Working slowly in the cover of the animals, each man took a halter and led Billy and Kismet up and out of the narrow wash, dragging the water kegs and the pack saddle.

Mora was good with a rifle, but there was not enough of either man showing for him to get a decent shot without taking a chance of hitting his animals. Within two minutes they were out of sight beyond a bulge of the hill.

He watched for a few minutes, the August sun beating mercilessly on his back and head. While they were occupied with the animals and the gear, he had a sudden, desperate thought of making a sliding dash down from the cave and finding another hiding place.

Just then, the sun glinted off something at the crest of a hill some eighty yards away. Maybe a piece of mica, he thought, squinting in that direction. Then his heart fell. He could barely make out a slight movement. The reflection was from either field glasses or a short gun barrel. They were watching from cover. An escape attempt now was too dicey. The cave was his best defensive position for the time being. He'd rest a while and then slide out under cover of darkness. It was his only chance. It was two against one, but he was at least as well armed as they were. There was no point in sitting in this hole to let them wait him out. He'd come out fighting if need be.

He squirmed backward into the narrow opening, picked up his canteen, and shook it. About half full, he estimated. He was thirsty enough right now to gulp down the remaining quart. His only food was one small piece of beef jerky in his pocket. In addition, he had a few matches, his belt knife, loaded Marlin and Smith & Wesson, and a handful of cartridges. He was all right for the moment, but not prepared for an extended siege.

The bulging leather sacks on the floor and the chunks of sponge gold lying about had seemed so all-absorbing and important thirty minutes before. Now it was like cement around his feet. This yellow metal was what it was all about — the reason for his predicament. Then he shook his head to clear his mind. No! The gold was only incidental. It was about honor, integrity, and resisting evil — the very things that'd led him to the desert in the first place.

He gathered up the remaining loose gold and stowed it in one of the sacks, tightened the drawstrings, and set the bags in a corner. With a groan, he sat down and leaned against the wall. Several hours of hard digging had already taken their toll on his strength and the muscles of his arms and back. He took a deep breath, tilting his head back against the rock. He would rest and conserve his remaining energy. At the moment, two men outside had the upper hand and could pick him off at will if he tried to escape the cave.

Glancing toward the brown robes that contained the mortal dust of the Franciscans, he muttered: "*Padre*s, pray that I don't join you any time soon."

CHAPTER EIGHTEEN

"I told you to stay up there and keep watch!" Deraux snapped as Rivera came stumbling down the slope toward him. The westering sun still lacked three hours of reaching the horizon. "We'll trade off an hour at a time until dark."

"How can I guard without a gun?" Rivera whined.

"If you see him poke his head out of that cave, just holler and I'll take care of him." He patted the blistering hot metal of the new Winchester he'd bought at the Yuma Mercantile; he'd fired it only twice at jack rabbits during their ride north along the river. "You ain't gonna have no gun or knife while I'm around you," Deraux said.

"When will you begin to trust me, *señor?*"

Not until you're miles from me, you whining weasel, Deraux thought. Aloud, he said: "As soon as we get this man's gold, we'll split up, and you can go wherever you want.

Since you're now wanted for that robbery and torture at Sand Tank station, you won't be trying to collect any reward on me by tipping off the law."

"We cannot wait for Mora to give up," Rivera said. "He could be telling the truth that he has much food and water in that cave. We could be here for a week."

Deraux had considered that possibility already.

"Someone has found Lila Strunk and her hostler by now. A deputy marshal from Tucson must be on our trail," Rivera continued. "And that clerk in the Yuma Mercantile. . . . I could tell by the way he looked at you . . . he knew you were one of the escaped prisoners. A posse might ride in on us at any moment."

"You want to skedaddle outta here and leave a fortune in that cave?" Deraux asked. "Go ahead."

"No. I want to go in and kill him and not waste any more time. What good is gold, if you can't get away to spend it?"

"I may be an outlaw, but I've never murdered a man."

Rivera flashed him a startled, disbelieving look.

"Killed two men in self-defense years ago," Deraux qualified his statement. "Not to say there couldn't be a third, unless you follow my orders," he added. "Now get back up that hill and stand your watch. One more day in there, and he'll be ready to make a deal . . . his life for the gold."

"What if he slips out tonight in the darkness?" Rivera demanded.

"All the better. Then we can have the gold to ourselves."

"We will not be safe as long as that man is alive and loose."

"You really hate him, don't you?"

"An arrogant *gringo* who took my job for his damned Indian!" He spat to one side. "He treated me like a dirty *peón* . . . like a pile of horse dung. Angel Rivera does not forget such insults!"

An idea was dawning in Deraux's mind. "If you're so dead set against this Mora, why don't you sneak up to that rat hole before daylight and carve him up with your favorite blade while he's still asleep?" Grinning, he pulled the Mexican's long, thin knife from his belt and held it up, taunting him. *With any luck, these two bastards will kill each other,* Deraux was thinking. *This man is a natural coward. I'll have to goad him into it.*

A wolfish look overcame Rivera's dark, narrow face. "I will take a *pistola,* also . . .

just in case."

"No you won't. You could turn it on me."

"But he is armed."

"Skeered of a tired old man?" Deraux taunted.

Rivera's face flushed even darker. "If I kill heem, I take a bigger share of the gold."

"Vengeance will be *your* reward. The gold will be split fifty-fifty."

Rivera licked his lips and his glance darted toward the knife and the Winchester.

Deraux knew he must never relax his vigilance. He had all the weapons — the two Colts, the rifle, and the knife. The only way he'd been able survive Rivera's hatred this long was to tie up the Mexican every night, and still sleep with one eye open. He would've run the man off long ago, except that he didn't favor watching his own back while he worked alone to find Mora's mine. Better to have this murderous greaser in plain sight at all times. "Get back on watch," he ordered. "I'll relieve you shortly so you can cook up some grub for supper. You'd best be ready for tonight."

Daniel Mora's eyes blinked open. For several seconds he didn't know where he was. Then it came back in a rush, and he wondered how long he'd been asleep. In spite of his resolve to remain alert, sleep had stolen over him. It was nearly dark in the cave. He took his Marlin and crawled slowly out the narrow opening, aware that someone might have a rifle trained on the gap between the rocks, waiting for him to show his head so it could be blown off.

But everything was still, with no sign of a watcher on the hillcrest. It was much lighter outside. The sun had disappeared, settling a peaceful, lingering twilight over the heated desert mountains. Maybe the two robbers were actually going to wait him out. Should he give up and let them have the mine in exchange for the water and his animals? He could fire a shot and wave his shirt to draw their attention. But he had no assurance he wouldn't be murdered as soon as he surrendered. They could hardly afford to let him carry his tale to the law.

He savored several deep breaths of the dry, aromatic desert air, then inched his way back inside. Should he eat the beef jerky to keep up his strength? Or would it make him even thirstier? It wasn't a hard decision. He pulled out the stiff, dried meat, brushed off the lint, and began gnawing at it. He washed it down with a pint of water, saving the last pint for a final drink before dawn when he'd risk everything on one roll of the dice. The gold would remain until he got clear and brought back some help. Even if these two outlaws got away with the full bags, they couldn't travel fast in this heat carrying all that weight. A swift posse with a tracker could catch up with them.

As darkness filled the cave, Mora struck a match and looked around to see if there might be some crevice where he could hide the bags. The space was only about eighteen by eight, and afforded no hiding place.

The match flickered out and he once more sat down, facing the opening. He set his mental clock to awaken him in the predawn hours, and relaxed with his Marlin across his lap.

He awoke several times during the long hours of darkness, neck and shoulders stiff. Uncorking his canteen, he drank the last pint of water. Then he shifted positions to relieve his legs on the hard floor, and dozed again, leaning against the rock.

Sometime later he dreamed of Lila Strunk. She was offering him a cool drink of spring water from a gourd as he sat on the bench outside Sand Tank station. A shadowy figure crept up behind her. Mora's voice seemed paralyzed and he couldn't shout a warning.

He gasped and jerked awake. In an instant he knew he wasn't alone. He smelled some animal presence, and rolled to his left, working the lever of his Marlin. Even as he cocked the carbine, something landed on him and a searing pain lanced across the top of his left shoulder. He reflexively squeezed the trigger and the explosion in the confined space was deafening. The brilliant muzzle flash showed a glimpse of a man with a knife. Hot, foul breath puffed into Mora's face. With a sudden lunge, Mora broke free and pivoted out from under the wiry body, instinctively thrusting up the carbine with both hands to ward off a second blow he knew was coming. An arm slammed down across the gun barrel in the dark and the knife clanged away on the floor. Mora jabbed the stock upward with all his strength and felt it glance off the man's head. His attacker screamed and threw himself into the battle once more. Grappling by feel in the darkness, Mora got to his knees and used leverage to tackle the man around the body and throw him over on his back. He was fighting for his life, and knew it. Warm blood coursed down his chest, his left arm rapidly losing strength.

Suddenly Mora felt a hand yank the Smith & Wesson from his belt. He let go and flung himself to one side. The pistol flashed and roared. The bullet missed, but a ricochet burned a red-hot groove along his right hip. For an instant, Mora saw the position of his attacker and grabbed for the gun arm with both hands. He clutched the bony wrist and forced the arm upward and back, bending the man's wrist so he was unable to cock the weapon again. Mora's left arm was going numb and he had to hold on with his right hand only. With a wrestler's move, he threw his legs around the slender man in a scissor grip, squeezing with all his strength. *Whoosh!* The air went out of the man like a flattened balloon. Mora sensed he had the advantage. Ignoring the pain in his hip, he released the scissor grip, crouched, and sprang to his feet, wrenching the pistol out of the man's hand as he did so. The Smith & Wesson clattered to the floor, and Mora suddenly realized he could make out the form of his opponent in the gray dawn light seeping into the cave. It was Rivera.

Mora's lungs were heaving and he paused for a second — a second that was nearly fatal. The Mexican sprang, catlike, snatched the knife from the floor, and, in one fluid motion, hurled it underhanded at Mora. The blade struck a rib and the knife cartwheeled away. Enraged by the piercing pain, Mora grabbed Rivera's arm, whipped the man around in a complete circle, and flung him across the room. The Mexican slammed backward into the wall, his head striking the projecting rock with the sound of a thumping watermelon. Rivera crumpled in a heap.

Mora leaned forward on his knees, gasping, slowly becoming conscious of pain in a dozen places. The acrid smell of burnt gunpowder irritated his dry throat. Several minutes it took for him to regain his breath before he limped forward to check the Mexican. He was dead. As the light grew stronger, Mora could make out dark blood staining a nugget of bright gold quartz lying beside the crushed skull.

He shoved his Smith & Wesson under his belt, then grabbed Rivera by one foot and dragged him, slowly and painfully, to the cave entrance. He shoved the body out through the narrow opening, and kept pushing until it tumbled off the ledge, landing with a thud thirty feet below in the narrow cañon. Then Mora crawled out and stood upright, taking a mighty breath. He pressed a hand to his left upper arm, realizing his shirt was wet with blood. The bleeding had nearly stopped, but his arm tingled as if there might be some nerve damage. Where was the other man? Mora knew he couldn't stand another *mano a mano*. If Rivera's partner — was Deraux his name? — showed up, they'd have to duel it out with guns. His adrenaline was ebbing and he felt queasy, but he knew he would survive. He looked at the light now touching the tops of the hills and felt a glow of optimism that over-whelmed the sting of his wounds.

On the crest of a ridge eighty yards away, made invisible by the rising sun at his back, Hugh Deraux lined up Mora in the open sights of his Winchester. Now that Rivera was out of the picture, all Deraux had to do was put a slug into Mora, load up all three mules and one burro with gold, water kegs, and food, and disappear. Within a few days, vultures, wolves, and coyotes would strip the bodies and scatter the bones. But, if anyone happened along before then, they would naturally conclude these two men had killed each other. A perfect set-up.

He worked the lever to put a cartridge into the chamber, then drew a bead on the chest of the dark, erect figure on the ledge. The man stood gazing toward the east, making a splendid target. One shot would do it. He held his breath and his finger tightened on the trigger, taking up the slack. He hesitated. Fifteen seconds passed. The barrel began to waver. He carefully let down the hammer with his thumb, and lowered the weapon. There was only one thing wrong with his plan. He couldn't murder a defenseless man. It was not in him. A low-down stage and gold robber he might be, but he was not a killer. Perhaps he should shoot Mora in the leg, then go down and help himself to whatever loose gold was handy. But wounding a solitary man out here was tantamount to killing him. No, he'd take the water and grub and let the merciless desert kill Mora, as it'd nearly killed him. *When his bones are bleaching, I'll come back and take the gold from that cave,* he thought. He doubted anyone would stumble across the mine during the remaining months of torrid heat. By winter, any manhunt for him would be abandoned. Patience was the key. Now was not the time to be greedy. Greed had tripped up many an outlaw. He was beginning to feel that instinctive twitch between his shoulder blades that told him Rivera was right — the law was not far away. Time to cut and run.

He slid back off the skyline and cat-footed a half mile to his camp. Working quickly, he saddled the mule he'd ridden in. He poured the remaining water into one keg, sacked up all the food he could find, and collected the camp gear. Then, cinching the pack saddle onto Rivera's mule, he tied on the load, taking care to stow under the bedroll the small sacks of gold they'd taken from Lila Strunk. This rich ore would be sufficient to get him started on some new life well away from Arizona Territory — provided he could reach a town with a stage line running east. He'd need to stash the ore in leather valises to look like normal luggage. A bath, shave, and new clothes and he'd blend in again. Although still rather short, his hair had grown out enough to lie down. Regretfully he couldn't take a chance on selling the branded mules. He'd dump their gear in the desert and turn the animals loose.

Plans for his eventual escape continued to churn through Hugh Deraux's head while the sun rose over the deserted hills. He mounted up and rode north, leading his loaded pack mule.

Nearly an hour later, an Indian on foot padded silently into the narrow cañon. Thirty yards behind followed a rider walking his Arabian mount. Quanto jogged forward as Coopersmith was startled when a half dozen black vultures flapped up heavily from the cañon floor at their approach. The Indian paused and pointed silently at the dark figure of a man hanging partly over the lip of a ledge above and about forty yards ahead. The Englishman's heart sank. They were too late.

Then Quanto loped ahead and hunkered beside a crumpled body at the base of the wall. That's what the buzzards were after, Coopersmith realized as he urged his horse forward and looked down. The big birds had not been at their work long and the face was still recognizable. It was Angel Rivera.

Coopersmith jerked a thumb at the arm of a man hanging over the ledge above them. Quanto leaped up, nimbly scaling the nearly vertical wall, picking hand and footholds, clambering up while loose rock and shale clattered down behind him. Coopersmith sat his horse and watched until the Indian reached the limp figure and turned him over. "Mora!" Quanto called.

"Dead?"

"No."

Coopersmith dismounted and ground-reined the Arabian and began what, for him, was a laborious ascent of the slightly inclined wall, slipping and sliding, skinning his shins. He finally pulled himself up onto the ledge, breathing heavily in the heat. He crouched by Mora and felt his pulse. He was breathing, but unconscious. Apparently he'd lost a lot of blood. Dirt and sand were caked on the half-dried blood on his clothing.

"Let's get him out of the sun, and see where he's wounded." He looked about quickly. Getting him off this ledge would be a problem without rope or something to anchor it to.

"Coop!" Quanto motioned for him to put his hand by an opening in the rock five feet away that was emitting cool air. The Indian got down and crawled on hands and knees into the mouth of the cave.

Coopersmith followed and stood up inside the ventilated room where a shaft of sunlight slanted down from an overhead crack some twenty feet above. He motioned for Quanto to drag Mora inside. The wounded man opened his eyes as he was being moved.

"Ah, two old friends," he muttered weakly.

At least he's in his right senses, Coopersmith thought. He cradled the injured man's head and held a canteen to his lips. "Rest easy. Where are you hurt?"

"Top of left arm, cut on the rib, bullet in the side of my buttock. Arm's the worst."

"We got here too late to warn you," the Englishman said. "Saw Rivera's body down below. Must have been one helluva fight."

Mora nodded. "Don't know where the

other man is."

"Your camp nearby?"

"About a mile to the north," he whispered huskily, accepting another drink of water.

"We'll clean you up as best we can here, then use your coil of rope to let you down the bluff," the Englishman said, planning as he spoke. "Think you can stand it?"

"Yeh."

"I want to get some hot coffee into you . . . and a little food when you can tolerate it. We'll take you to camp and bandage those wounds."

"I'm mostly just sore."

Coopersmith glanced around and saw the mummified Franciscans for the first time. "My God, what's that?"

"Tell you about it later." He gestured weakly with his head. "Vein of gold back there in the wall. Got a couple bags full of ore."

Quanto came over and hunkered by him, taking out his knife to begin cutting off the bloody shirt.

Mora struggled to sit up and assist him. "Quanto, this is the third time you've come to my rescue. Now I finally have the means to thank you."

If the Tarahumara understood, his stony expression never changed. "No talk. Rest."

CHAPTER NINETEEN

November 3, 1878
Sand Tank Station

"That's the last of it," Jason Watley said. "We're packed and ready."

"Thanks, Jason. Better have a last look around to make sure we didn't forget anything," Lila Strunk said.

The hostler disappeared inside the log building where Quanto and Coopersmith were tying up their bedrolls from having slept on the plank floor overnight. Sand Tank station was now officially closed. Hired wranglers had retrieved the stagecoach company's livestock three days before.

Lila's few belongings were packed on the wagon.

"I hate to leave this place," she said. "It's been home for some years now, and Frank is buried here." She wore a wistful look as her gaze rested on the buildings and the cottonwoods.

Daniel Mora nodded. "I thought you might be here at least until the railroad reached Tucson . . . maybe another sixteen months."

"Yes." She nodded. "But business was off, and the stage company decided to go ahead and shut down."

"I'm surprised at that, since the Southern Pacific only resumed construction this week. Quanto left them just before they halted building for three months because of the heat and lack of wooden ties."

Lila shrugged. "They won't even reach Casa Grande until next spring."

"I reckon the S.P. saved a few dollars by routing the line several miles south," Mora said. "They apparently don't need this spring for the steam engines."

"The spring is what I'm going to miss most about this place," Lila said. "I'm afraid the station'll be abandoned and the Indians will reclaim it."

"Nobody will own the water, though. Sand Tank Spring will be like all the other springs in the desert . . . it'll belong to the animals and any traveler who wants to use it." He looked at Lila who was dressed in a long, blue traveling dress, her graying hair swept up and pinned under a wide-brimmed matching hat. He'd urged her to take his Smith & Wesson for protection, and she'd tucked it into her handbag, which she'd placed on the bench while they talked. Dressed up like this, she appeared ten years younger than when he'd last seen her. "I probably won't come back this way," he said after a short silence. "It'll seem too desolate without you."

"Where do you go from here?"

It was the question Daniel Mora had been dreading, and he was glad Lila wasn't looking directly at him when she asked it.

"Not real sure," he answered truthfully.

"No thought of returning to San Francisco?"

He shook his head. "No. But who can say what's down the road? Times change . . . people change."

"If you go back to that woman, you're a fool."

He laughed. "Lila, I can always count on you for an unbiased opinion."

"Living out here has ground all the subtlety out of me. It's reduced my life to the essentials."

For the last time they stood near the gurgling spring outside the station. The morning sun was an hour above the horizon, dispelling the overnight autumn chill.

Her distressed expression melted into a smile. "Now that you've endowed all your friends with a passel of gold, you'd best decide what you're going to do with what's left." While he was fashioning some appropriate reply, she went on: "You can't escape responsibility by hiding in the desert, you know."

"I took your advice and registered the claim," he said.

"A good first step."

"And I sent enough to my wife to keep her for the rest of her years."

"Not that she deserves it." Lila sniffed.

"Most of us don't get what we deserve, for better or worse. And I, for one, am glad of it."

"You're probably right," she acknowledged. "The sun and rain fall equally on the good and the bad. I'd rather have the Almighty's mercy than His justice." She glanced toward the span of mules harnessed to the spring wagon that would haul her and the hostler to Tucson. From there she planned to travel on to live with her widowed sister in Cincinnati.

"You know, you and I would have made a wonderful couple," she said quietly. "We've both traveled some hard roads and don't have any unrealistic expectations."

"Lila, I love you," he said simply, touching the barely visible scars on her neck. "If my wife should die. . . ."

She shook her head. "You're entirely too straight-laced, Dan. Even if that lady you're parted from should pass away, you and I'll never get together. Once we leave here, we'll go our own ways and never see each other again. That's just the way of things, and we both know it."

Making no reply, Mora turned aside and took a long, slow breath, savoring the musical trill of an unseen warbler cheering the desert morning. The warmth of the sun through the branches of the cottonwood felt good on his back; only a few months before he would have dreaded the coming of the day's blistering heat.

"Do your wounds still bother you?" she finally asked.

"No. They're completely healed. I may not be good as new" — he grinned — "but I'm as good as slightly used."

"What's next?" she asked again.

"I've taken Quanto and Coopersmith as partners in the mine," Mora said, "so now there are four of us. You get half, per our agreement, and the other half will be divided three ways."

"Dan, I don't want all that," she insisted

again. "I'll settle for what's in that strongbox you brought me."

"Nevertheless, I've got your sister's address in Ohio. You'll be hearing from me as the mine develops. Quanto, Coopersmith, and I will dig out what we can during the mild winter months, and then decide if the Saint Francis is worth keeping. Should the vein start to pinch out, or go too deep, we might sell to some big mining company that has the equipment and expertise to do hard-rock tunneling. The three of us get along well and can work together. Coopersmith will have time to finish his book, and we can teach Quanto more English."

"If that Indian shares his gold with his people, he'll have the richest village in the Sierra Madre," Lila said, and laughed.

"Come next summer, if we've sold the mine, I'll probably donate a good chunk of my money to charity, then go live in a cooler climate for a few months. But I'll come back to the desert. It's part of me . . . like the salt in my blood. Can't really explain it. Eternal . . . peaceful."

"I know. I won't stay away long, either. Maybe I can convince my sister the dry, warm climate would help her rheumatism."

"In a couple more generations," he said, "this whole country will likely be civilized and settled."

She was silent for a few moments. "What did you do with those two mummies you found?" she asked.

"Brought them in caskets to Yuma for a belated funeral Mass. They're buried in the churchyard. It was time they got a little rest after guarding that mine for a hundred years. The parish priest there is doing some research in the Spanish records to find out who they were."

"And the law hasn't caught up with Hugh Deraux yet?" she inquired.

"Not yet. Frankly I don't care if they ever do. He's gone out of our lives."

Coopersmith and Quanto emerged, and the Englishman tied his bedroll behind the California saddle. Lila had made him a present of the Arabian, Pistol. Since Quanto still wasn't used to riding a horse, Mora had stabled his mule and burro, and they'd traveled here from Yuma in a light, rented buggy. They all gathered to give Lila her share of gold, and to help her pack to leave.

Jason came outside to join them. "The place is cleaned out," the hostler announced.

The men shook hands with Jason and hugged Lila. Mora was last and kissed her. He held her close for several seconds and could feel her heart beating. It was a sensation he would remember for a long time. When they pulled apart, her eyes were moist. She brushed away a tear that escaped onto her cheek. "Daniel Mora, look what you've done to me," she said.

The hostler climbed to the driver's seat of the wagon and Mora helped Lila up on the other side. A metal strongbox packed with a generous amount of rich sponge gold rested in the bed of the wagon along with her luggage. Mora had no worries about her being alone with this hostler. He was an honorable man if Mora'd ever seen one. And Lila had the loaded pistol in her bag, just in case.

Coopersmith mounted his horse. Mora and Quanto climbed into the buggy. With a last wave Mora pulled the horse around and snapped the reins over its back. He didn't see Lila looking over her shoulder as Jason drove their team out onto the Gila Road and headed toward the rising sun.

ABOUT THE AUTHOR

Tim Champlin, born John Michael Champlin in Fargo, North Dakota, was graduated from Middle Tennessee State University and earned a Master's degree from Peabody College in Nashville, Tennessee. Beginning his career as an author of the Western story with *Summer of the Sioux* in 1982, the American West represents for him "a huge, ever-changing block of space and time in which an individual had more freedom than the average person has today. For those brave, and sometimes desperate souls who ventured West looking for a better life, it must have been an exciting time to be alive." Champlin has achieved a notable stature in being able to capture that time in complex, often exciting, and historically accurate fictional narratives. He is the author of two series of Westerns novels, one concerned with Matt Tierney who comes of age in *Summer of the Sioux* and who begins his professional career as a reporter for the *Chicago Times-Herald* covering an expeditionary force venturing into the Big Horn country and the Yellowstone, and one with Jay McGraw, a callow youth who is plunged into outlawry at the beginning of *Colt Lightning.* There are six books in the Matt Tierney series and with *Deadly Season* a fifth featuring Jay McGraw. In *The Last Campaign,* Champlin provides a compelling narrative of Geronimo's last days as a renegade leader. *Swift Thunder* is an exciting and compelling story of the Pony Express. *Wayfaring Strangers* is an extraordinary story of the California Gold Rush. In all of Champlin's stories there are always unconventional plot ingredients, striking historical details, vivid characterizations of the multitude of ethnic and cultural diversity found on the frontier, and narratives rich and original and surprising. His exuberant tapestries include lumber schooners sailing the West Coast, early-day wet-plate photography, daredevils who thrill crowds with gas balloons and the first parachutes, tong wars in San Francisco's Chinatown, Basque sheepherders, and the *Penitentes* of the Southwest, and are always highly entertaining.

We hope you have enjoyed this Large Print book. Other Thorndike, Wheeler, Kennebec, and Chivers Press Large Print books are available at your library or directly from the publishers.

For information about current and upcoming titles, please call or write, without obligation, to:

Publisher
Thorndike Press
295 Kennedy Memorial Drive
Waterville, ME 04901
Tel. (800) 223-1244

or visit our Web site at:

http://gale.cengage.com/thorndike

OR

Chivers Large Print
published by AudioGO Ltd
St James House, The Square
Lower Bristol Road
Bath BA2 3SB
England
Tel. +44(0) 800 136919
email: info@audiogo.co.uk
www.audiogo.co.uk

All our Large Print titles are designed for easy reading, and all our books are made to last.